BISHOP

RM JOHNSON

Published by **MarcusArts, LLC**

This is a work of fiction. Names, characters, businesses, places, events and incidents are either the products of the author's imagination or used

BISHOP

By

RM JOHNSON

Marcusarts LLC—Atlanta, GA

1

The windows were dark in his bedroom when little Larry woke from his sleep to the sound of yelling. Wearing Sesame Street pajamas, he climbed down from bed and walked the narrow hallway to the living room.

He stopped silent in the doorway when he saw his father, Lincoln, pulling on his mother's arm, attempting to stop her from exiting the open front door.

"Why you gotta leave? Things gonna get better!" Lincoln promised. He was tall, broad shouldered, thin with sinewy muscles.

The clock on the living room wall read 2:30 a.m., but Larry's mother, Cynthia, had her hair fixed in big curls and her face made up like she had somewhere special to go. She wore knee-high boots and a thigh-high skirt. What disturbed Larry most was the two beaten up, purple suitcases that sat at his mother's feet. She tried yanking away from her husband, but Lincoln held tight to her.

"Mamma...where you going?" Little Larry asked, wiping sleep from his eyes.

Cynthia turned to Lincoln. "Now look what you did." She picked up both bags, turned and tried to push through the closed screen door in front of her. Lincoln grabbed her, more forcefully than before, causing both bags to fall from her hands

"You just gonna walk out with your boy standing right there in front of you? Ain't even gonna answer his question."

"Mamma, you leaving?" Larry asked. He was only eight and half years old, but he heard their arguments at night behind their bedroom door. The mornings after, he'd always see his father searching the want ads for jobs with a red pen. He'd go out hopeful in the mornings and come back hopeless in the evening. Larry figured this had something to do with that.

"Answer the boy!" Lincoln demanded.

Cynthia shook her head. "Go back to bed, Larry!" his mother said, only glancing at him.

"Mamma, why you leaving us?" A tear spilled over Larry's eye and ran down his face.

"Larry, go to bed, now!" Cynthia ordered.

"Tell us why you leavin'!" Lincoln said. "Things are hard, but they gonna get better."

Cynthia narrowed her eyes on her husband. "Things more than hard. How long until they foreclose on the house, Lincoln? How long until the car out front gets fixed after sitting there for two months? How long till you get a job after being off thirteen months? We behind on every bill," Cynthia said, wiping around her mascara at the tears that clouded her eyes. "Ain't no food in the kitchen, and how many times Larry gone to bed hungry the past week?"

Lincoln stood mute in front of his wife, his grip loosening.

"Say something!" Cynthia screamed. To Larry she sounded nearly hysterical. "Tell me! Tell your son. How things gonna get better?" Cynthia brushed her husband's hand from her arm, kneeled, opened her arms and called her son over. Little Larry ran into his mother's embrace, squeezing her tight. He sobbed heavily on her shoulder then immediately felt her pushing him away. "You be good," was all she said then kissed him on the cheek before grabbing her bags.

"And you just gonna leave us here? Abandon your son for—" Lincoln started.

"You want me to take him?" Cynthia said, "Because I—"

"No!" Lincoln said, grabbing his son by the shoulder and pulling him close. "Leave all you want, but you ain't takin' my boy," Lincoln said, his forearm pressed so heavily over Larry's chest that he felt pain.

"Fine," Cynthia said, staring sadly at her son. "Take good care of him." She threw the strap of one of the old bags over her shoulder, grabbed the other, then turned on her high heels, pushed through the screen door and was gone.

"Mamma!" Larry cried, trying to follow her, but his father held him back. Lincoln turned his son around to face him, and with big, dry hands, smeared the tears from Larry's cheeks. "She's gone boy, but we gonna be all right, you hear me?"

Larry couldn't answer he was so hurt by his mother's abandonment.

"I love you!" Lincoln said, holding Larry by his shoulders. "Do you love me?"

Larry nodded, and spoke so softly his voice could barely be heard. "Yeah."

"Do you love me, boy?" His father spoke louder, shaking Larry.

"Yeah Daddy, I love you!" Larry said, frightened by the fear he saw in his father's wide eyes.

"Good. Then we got enough love between us to make everything all right."

Larry Lakes lay in bed, forty-two years later, bare-chested on his back, staring unblinking at the ceiling. Muscular, brown skinned and bearded with a skull he kept cleanly shaved, he tried to forgive himself for visiting his painful past again. It was almost impossible to do.

His wife Marian lay beside him, her back to him. She moaned then whined two words he could not understand. She had been doing that the past couple of nights.

Larry peeled back the blanket, careful not to wake her. Wearing pajama bottoms,
he lowered himself to his knees at the side of the bed, pressed his palms together, closed his eyes and prayed.

"I do not fear this day, for you are with me wherever I might go your light to shine ahead, your footsteps to lead the way. I do not fear this day for your word will be my guide, your strength will sustain me, your love revive me this day and all days. I do not fear this day for you are with me." He opened his eyes slowly, breathed in deeply and exhaled. "Amen."

2

"You sleep okay?" Larry asked, as Marian stood before him knotting his necktie. He stared over her shoulder at the local morning news.

"Yeah, why do you ask?" Marian was a beautiful woman of 5'3", her straightened black hair cut shoulder length. She wore only enough makeup—eyeliner and lipstick—to accent her big eyes and full lips. She looked much younger than her forty years.

"Just asking," Larry said. "You were tossing and turning and talking in your sleep."

"Really?" Marian laughed nervously. "Make out what I was saying?"

"Unh uh," Larry said, losing interest in the exchange. His eyes were on the news again. The report was about him. Images of last Saturday's "anti-gay" march played across the screen. Larry watched himself marching down the center of 10th Street, bordering Piedmont Park. It was the heart of Atlanta's gay district, where rainbow colored flags flew and same sex couples strolled hand in hand. Larry marched boldly, shoulder-to-shoulder, surrounded by members from his thirty thousand-member congregation, all of them chanting, "Hey, hey, you weren't born that way! Hey, hey, you weren't born this way!" They were referring to the scores of gay, lesbian and transgender people who lined the curbs, holding homemade picket signs, angrily shouting back, pumping their fists, showing their unrestrained disapproval for the display of intolerance.

In their bedroom, Larry felt Marian release the ends of his tie to step around him, grab the remote off the foot of the bed and aim it at the TV. Larry caught her by the wrist and eased the remote from her hand.

"That's over now, Larry," Marian said. "You don't have to watch that."

"People still talking about it. The church is still suffering for it, so I need to see what they see."

The march was Larry's idea. But it wasn't his intention to offend those people. He wanted to help them, make them aware that there was an alternative, that they could be cured if they just came to him for help.

Larry thumbed up the volume so he could hear the reporter.

"—and there is still fallout from the controversial march organized by the Bishop Larry Lakes of Holy Sweet Spirit Church."

Larry hit the mute button then angrily tossed the remote to the unmade bed. "Are you done with this?" He asked looking down at the tie his wife had not completed knotting. She quickly finished the task. Larry thanked her.

"Was it that bad? Did I offend that many people?" he asked.

"I don't know what you're talking about," Marian said. "You were only trying to help."

Larry considered what she said, his eyes lowering, observing the sheer, black nightgown she wore. It easily displayed her full, round breasts underneath—her attempt to persuade him to make love to her last night. It did not work.

"The march," Larry said. "What everyone is calling the "anti-gay march." It wasn't anti-gay. It was about that fact that in God's eyes, marriage is still just between a man and a woman. Obviously, people don't understand. You've seen the congregation over the last several

9

Sundays. It's getting smaller. We're losing money. So much that the accountant called yesterday, talking about it's urgent I see him. Does it have anything to do with that march, with the message I've been giving?"

Marian took Larry by the hand. "Sweetheart, you're the bishop of that church. You built it from the ground up, grew that ministry from three hundred followers to thirty thousand. How can anything you say be wrong?"

Larry stared into Marian's face, searched deep into her eyes for deception of any

kind. He smiled, pulled his wife close and kissed her cheek.

"Okay, darling. Maybe you're right."

3

Marian showered in her private bathroom inside the huge Buckhead mansion. It had six bedrooms, an indoor swimming pool and four Doric Roman columns out front, overlooking a circular driveway. It was the home Larry had bought the family seven years ago, before the housing bubble burst. Marian told him they didn't need so much space, so much opulence; he could save his money and buy a smaller place. Larry laughed and without concern, told her he was making more money than they'd ever spend. Going by what her husband just told her, there was a lot less money now, and a lot more concern.

But Marian loved the house, and she loved her bathroom. The mansion had five of them. Larry had his own, each of their kids, Jabari, their son, eight years old, and Simone, their daughter, six, had one of their own, complete with marble vanities, heated floors and Jacuzzi bathtubs.

Marian turned around letting the hot water hit her face. She sponged under her arms with the shower gel Larry had given to her yesterday. It cost forty dollars per eight-ounce tube. "Whatever it costs, only the best for my wife," he always said, and Marian couldn't help but think the gift was just a small fraction of what she would receive tonight for their tenth wedding anniversary. She was looking forward to it, as she was sure Larry was, even though he hadn't discussed what he had planned for them.

Just like last year and the three before, it was a game he played, showing up in the evening, dressed in a sharp suit to whisk her away for a night filled with fine food, drink, entertainment and gifts.

Marian could hardly believe it had been ten years.

A couple of those had been a struggle, especially the last one, but as one of the bible scriptures said, *love never fails*. She thought it was Corinthians. It was the one she had been reminding herself of a lot lately because although she and Larry hardly made love anymore, she still loved and was devoted to her husband. But as she turned and let the hot water massage her back, she asked herself how truly devoted she was if last night she dreamt of another man.

Since undressing and stepping into the shower, Marian had tried to shake the sensual thoughts, but his beautiful, muscular body, the strength with which he held his forearm around her neck, tightening the lock just enough to make her heart race—made the thoughts impossible to ignore. In her dream last night she wore no clothes, was on her knees. He had forced her down there after fighting her clothes off. He tore his away and came up behind her, pressed his warm body to hers, snaking his forearm around her neck, slipping his other hand underneath her, between her legs. He slipped his hot wet tongue into her ear and whispered, "Don't move. Just take what I'm about to do to you." He massaged the soft folds between her thighs until her head spun, her limbs went weak and she moaned, "No, no! I can't take it!" She felt her juices running over his hand, down the insides of her trembling, weakening thighs. She felt her arms and legs were going to give any moment, and she tried to fight him off. He held her steady, spreading the cheeks of her behind. She glanced over her shoulder, saw his muscular figure covered in beautiful dark skin, his penis erect, his hand slowly, sensually gliding up its length. She turned away, unable to believe what was happening, what she was allowing to happen. She stacked her forearms, lowered her cheek against them, closing her eyes, preparing to be entered, and savor—

A loud knock came at the bathroom door. "Mamma! Pops said come down for breakfast before he has to leave."

Marian was startled out of her thoughts, one hand between her legs, the other cupped her left breast as steam wafted up from the hot water spraying her.

"Okay, Jabari. Be down in a sec," Marian said, her heart racing, her voice quivering. She punched the big button that shut off the showerhead. Leaning against the shower wall, she pressed her head to her forearm, wondering what would've happened if she allowed a dream like that to become a reality? What would've happened if she had called the name of the man in the dream and her husband heard her?

Downstairs, Estelle, Marian's mother, a regal-looking woman of sixty-six, with a broad nose and high forehead, scooped more bacon onto her granddaughter Simone's plate. Estelle wore her salt and pepper hair cropped close on the sides and back of her head and curled on top. She wore a pastel purple St. John's slacks suit with low-heeled matching shoes.

"Easy with the bacon, Ma," Marian said.

"It's turkey bacon," Estelle said. "It won't hurt the girl."

"That's right, Mommy. It won't hurt the girl," Simone said, crunching down on one of the strips Estelle gave her. Simone's hair was parted down the middle, two
shiny pigtails with purple barrettes dangling from the ends, hung from either side of the girl's head.

A tall, handsome brown-skinned man stood back in a corner of the large kitchen, wearing a light colored suit and a simple smile. He had not taken his eyes off Marian since she entered the room.

Marian tried to ignore his gaze, thought to ask him what the hell was he staring at, but told herself she would deal with him later. She nervously looked up at Larry to see if he had noticed the man's fascination with his wife. He had not. He was consumed in conversation with his son, as he often was.

Jabari, who was thin and a little taller than the average kid his age, wore glasses to correct his horrible vision. He was gawky, and a bit awkward looking, but Larry kept his hair neatly cut every week and Marian knew he would grow into a handsome man like his father.

Larry stood from his chair, mussed Jabari's hair, kissed his daughter on the cheek and said, "I'm about to get out here, Ma," Larry said to his mother-in-law. "You have a good day, do something nice for yourself on me. You deserve it."

Estelle forced a smile and waited till her son-in-law was not looking to roll her eyes. "Have a wonderful day, Larry."

Marian stood, received the hug and peck on the cheek her husband gave her. She held onto his arm as she felt him try to pull away. "You're going to make it back home at a decent time tonight, I hope," Marian smiled.

Larry looked at Marian if for the answer to a question different question from the one she posed, then said, "You know I'll do my best."

14

4

Robby Gentry checked his Timex, glanced over at the prison infirmary door then gave his attention to the blonde, male nurse in green scrubs, standing in front of him.

"Dude, you call the doctor?" Robby asked. "How long it take him to get here?"

The nurse said, "I called him ten minutes ago. He was at lunch, but he said he'd be here as soon as he can."

Robby looked up at the inmate next to him. To Robby he seemed surprisingly calm to have endured what he had. To the nurse, Robby said, "Can you do anything till the doc gets here?"

The nurse, his name was Ken, looked at the inmate, then shook his head. "Let's just wait. It won't be much longer."

"I'm cool," the inmate, a twenty-seven-year-old man named Treyshaun said. He wore a black stocking cap over his cornrowed hair and a white t-shirt under his open, button down prison shirt. Elaborate black tattoos snaked their way up the collar of his t-shirt and around his neck.

Robby felt as though he was suffering more than Treyshaun.

Half an hour ago, Robby walked up casually beside the inmate, took him by the elbow and said softly, "Come with me. You're bleeding."

Robby had noticed that the man who had just walked into the dayroom had a bloodstain the size of a softball in the seat of his pants. Robby would've questioned exactly what had happened, but Treyshaun was limping, seemingly trying to hide his discomfort. Robby had been a corrections officer for more than three years, and knew when he saw a rape victim. Unfortunately that wasn't the only familiarity he had with men raping men.

Robby called his supervisor, made him aware he was taking Treyshaun to the infirmary, then called to notify them he was coming.

Now, standing in the small treatment room still waiting for the doctor to show, Robby could hardly stand to look at the man again. He forced himself. "So, were you…you know?" Robby asked, knowing the answer.

Treyshaun, nodded. "Yeah, yesterday."

Treyshaun was huge, 6'5", and looked to have been built of 250 pounds of sheer muscle.

"But dude, you're a monster."

Treyshaun stared at the wall across the room. "Don't matter if five or six dudes holding you down."

Robby shut his eyes against the image. He fought to keep his mind in the present, fought the urge to feel sorry for himself for what he endured in the past. "Who did it?"

"Don't know."

"You do know."

Treyshaun glanced quickly at Robby then looked off again. "There were five or six of them motherfuckers. I was trying to save my ass, not remember faces. Even if I did know, why the fuck would I tell you?"

"Because I can do something about it."

"Yeah, file a report. Then I'm a snitch, and I'm getting fucked up the ass every night."

"You don't wanna get back at whoever did this to you?"

Treyshaun, his eyes still glazed over, said, his voice low, "Yeah, but I want the motherfuckers beat down."

"What do you think I was talking about?"

"You'd do that for me?" Treyshaun said, looking at Robby, something near gratitude in his eyes.

"You did something out on the streets that required you get locked up and do time as punishment, not get fucked by some grown as men. Nobody should have to suffer that. Tell me who did it?"

"I saw one face."

"Then he's the unlucky guy."

After the doctor came, Robby left the infirmary and made his way toward the exit of the prison to clear his head of what he just had to deal with. Walking down the long corridor that led outside, he saw a guard escorting a beautiful, young woman carrying a briefcase. She wore a dark business suit and sexy heals. She was an attorney. Her name was Shelia Kennedy and over the last six months, Robby had seen her there a few times every week. Each and every time he spotted her, he'd shoot a little game her way, try and make her smile in hopes of one day getting her number and asking her out.

As they neared each other, Robby smiled, but noticed Shelia look away as if she hadn't seen him.

Ten feet in front of Shelia, Robby smiled wider and said, "Attorney Kennedy, I'm gonna need you to represent me. I'm about to commit a crime."

"And what crime is that, Officer Gentry?" Shelia said, not slowing down as she continued on with the other corrections officer.

"Stealing your heart," Robby said.

17

"How about sexual harassment?" Shelia said, over her shoulder, with a smile.

Robby stood in the center of the hallway, staring at how her skirt clung to her hips and behind as she walked away. "Guilty as charged," Robby said to himself.

5

Larry sat in a large, glass walled conference room staring angrily at a seventeen- year-old black girl, the terrible financial news he had just gotten still swirling about in his head.

He had just come from the appointment with his accountant and was told that money just wasn't coming in like it used to.

"Donations from the congregation are down almost 40 percent from last year. Contributions from outside sources, down 25 percent," Marty Grayson, the blonde, middle-aged accountant said.

Larry didn't believe the situation was so dire that he had to ask the question that swirled in his head, but he needed the answer. "Are we making enough to keep the church?"

"Not much more," Marty said. "If this trend continues, with all due respect, you're going to be in a world of hurt."

Larry slowly stood from his chair, walked to the front of Marty's desk, leaned over it, resting his fingertips on it like a teepee. He wore big, jeweled rings on two of the fingers of each hand, as well as the diamond wedding band on his left. "And what are you telling me?" Larry asked.

"What you have in your business account now is enough to keep the lights on in the church, your mansion and your family fed. With the money that you're losing, you might want to consider liquidating a few things. One of the cars, maybe, one of the other houses, I don't know. You said the new church would make all sorts of money. What's going on with that?"

"City ordinances, zoning violations, red tape, I'm told," Larry said. "But I know it's the mayor stopping everything. The Union City church leaders are threatening him. I have a meeting with them this evening. Know that I'm going to get to the bottom of this."

"Well Bishop," Marty said, standing from his chair. "You're going to have to, because soon, not only will there not be any new church, you might have to close the doors of the old one."

Larry refocused his attention on the teenaged girl across from him. She was attractive with clear brown skin and bright, alert eyes, despite the hardships she was enduring. Larry knew of those hardships because this girl and her mother had been members of his church for the last three years.

The girl's name was Tatiana Benson. She was a member of the girl's ministry, and her mother often volunteered time around the church.

Tatiana's father had been laid off from his job at the automobile assembly plant two years ago, and things hadn't been going very well for the family since.

Larry was able to sympathize with her, remembering all the times his father Lincoln went without work, and the poverty they endured because of it. The suffering many nights without food, without shelter, some even without hope. Larry had promised himself every night, whether sleeping on a flattened cardboard box, wrapped up, hugging his father against the cold, or in an apartment they were temporarily able to afford, that he'd never go back to that life once he left it.

Tatiana Benson and her family had received financial help from the church on several occasions, as well as bags and boxes of food: a turkey for both Thanksgiving and Christmas, and gift cards for the local Kroger grocery store whenever Larry could get his hands on them. It was the reason he was so outdone by her sitting there across from him, her mother to Tatiana's left, a stern-faced, thin, dark haired attorney, to her right.

"Are you going to say something in regard to the accusations, Mr. Lakes?" Ms. Michaels, the Benson attorney said.

"That's Bishop Lakes," Tyrell Suggs said. He sat to Larry's left, his white driving cap on the table in front of him. Tyrell sidled up closer to the desk, wearing a dark, pinstriped suit. "The mans a Bishop. You need to be calling him that."

"I'm sorry," the attorney, Ms. Michaels said. "Do you have anything to say, Bishop Lakes?"

His chair turned sideways so that he could cross his legs and rest an elbow on the table, allowing him to hold his face in his hand while he stared at Tatiana's downturned eyes, Larry casually asked, "What are the accusations again?"

Ms. Michaels cleared her voice as though aggravated and said, "That on more than half a dozen occasions, while alone with Tatiana Benson, you made sexual advances toward her. More specifically, that you fondled her breasts, groped her while alone in one of the activity rooms, kissed her several times against her will, and forced her to perform oral sex on you."

"That is complete bullshit," Tyrell Suggs said under his breath.

"Sir, if you would please—" Ms. Michaels said.

"How could you?" Larry said, saddened by what the girl was charging him with.

"How could you?" Katrina, Tatiana's mother said, emotion forcing her voice to crack. She was near tears. "My child trusted you. I trusted you!" She stood from her chair, leaned over the table, pointing at Larry. "And you…and you do this!"

Tyrell Suggs stood up. "Sit down, lady."

"No, you sit down!" Mrs. Benson said.

"Sit down, Tyrell," Larry said, his voice calm and even.

Tyrell Suggs retook his seat.

Mrs. Benson did the same. Ms. Michaels reached over and patted her shoulder, making sure she was all right.

"If I did these things, why haven't you gone to the police?" Larry asked of Tatiana.

"Bishop, if you'd direct your questions to me," Ms. Michaels said.

Larry kept his eyes on the girl, noticing that she would not look at him, that she had only glanced at him once in the half hour they've been sitting across from each other.

"Fine," Larry said. "The question is for you then, Attorney Michaels."

"She hasn't gone to the police out of respect for you and concern for the church she loves. Tatiana wanted to give you the opportunity to address and settle this issue out of the public eye."

"Settle?" Larry said. "And exactly how would I do that?"

"Like I said earlier, Bishop, if you had brought your attorney like I had asked, this could—"

"And like I said earlier, Attorney Michaels, I didn't bring him because I knew I wouldn't need him. Not for this. Now if you'd just answer my question."

Ms. Michaels readjusted herself in her chair. "For pain and anguish suffered by Ms. Benson, a monetary settlement would have to be reached in order to keep this situation from going any further."

"Tatiana," Larry said, turning to the girl. "If it was money you needed all you had to do was come to me. I told you that. It's still not too late," Larry said, going into his suit jacket pocket and bringing out his checkbook. He set it on the table, opened it up, slid the pen from the binder, looked to Tatiana's mother and said, "Tell me how much you need? And I'm not talking about no settlement. How much do you do need for groceries and to pay a few bills? And later on if—"

"Bishop Lakes!" Ms. Michaels said. "We are not here for this, and that is no way to—"

"These are my people. They are part of my flock. I'm trying to help them out."

"Help?" Mrs. Benson said. "After what you did to us we don't want your help, and we are no longer part of your flock. We're never coming back to your church."

Considering the number of parishioners Larry had already lost and the money they took with them, that statement hurt him almost as much as Tatiana's false accusations.

Larry shook his head and exhaled. He closed the checkbook, slid it back into his jacket pocket then stood from the table. Tyrell Suggs stood after him, grabbing his hat.

"Well Ms. Michaels, Mrs. and Ms. Benson, I will not be blackmailed and forced into paying money for something I did not do," Larry said. He walked around the table toward the door, Tyrell Suggs following him.

"Bishop Lakes," Ms. Michaels said, standing. "If you do not deal with this, we will file charges and take this to trial."

"Do what you have to do, Ms. Michaels," Larry said, standing aside so Tyrell Suggs could open the door for him.

"But first the press will be informed of this," Ms. Michaels warned. "All of Atlanta, all of Georgia, the entire country will hear of this. Do you understand the damage it will do to your church, Bishop Lakes?"

Larry halted before walking out the open door. He knew, and it pained him to think of just how damaging it truly would be, how much more money his church may lose.

"Whoever dwells in the shelter of the Most High will rest in the shadow of the Almighty. I will say of the Lord, He is my refuge and my fortress, my God, in whom I trust." Larry displayed a smile, hoping it hid just how troubled he was. "What is being said of me cannot do me any harm if it is not true, Ms. Michaels. Have a blessed day."

6

Marian searched the rack of evening dresses at Neiman Marcus. She selected a black one with a plunging neckline and held it pressed against her torso as she looked herself in the mirror.

In the reflection, she saw Paul staring at her.

"What are you looking at?"

"I like that one," Paul said, taking a step forward. "What's the occasion?"

He had no business asking that. But he did a lot of things he had no business doing like gazing at her during breakfast this morning. She had addressed that issue with him as he chauffeured her over in the Lincoln Town Car.

"Why were you staring at me like that this morning?" She had asked from the back seat. She caught his eyes in the rearview mirror. They squinted into a smile, but he remained silent.

"You want to answer that or what?"

"I'm sorry. I didn't know I was staring this morning," Paul said, turning the big car into the underground parking lot of the store. "I won't do it again."

"That's right, you won't," Marian said, wondering just how long Paul would last working for her.

Six months ago, Barry, the older gentleman that had served Marian for the previous five years, retired. That's when Larry presented Marian with Paul Baker.

The man was handsome, well built, well-spoken and was too charismatic for his own good, but Marian only cared that he was qualified.

Looking at his resume then, she saw that he had been employed as a personal trainer, a bartender, a carpenter, a hotel concierge and a club bouncer.

"Man of many talents, huh," Marian said, peering over the top of the page at him.

He smiled that smile of straight, white teeth.

"Do you have references?"

"Your husband contacted them all. He has them."

"Fine," Marian said, staring hesitantly at Paul, feeling that there was something just not right about him. "I guess you start tomorrow."

The first three months of Paul's employment went very well. He was polite and cheerful, always greeting Marian in the morning when he came in to pick up the kids with a smile and a compliment about how lovely, young or radiant she looked—compliments her husband had stopped giving her years ago.

Marian noticed a strange energy whenever she was around him.

She had to ask herself was it something he was intentionally doing to her—was there something more he wanted of her than the job he held?

She had rudely discovered the answer a week later while she and Paul walked through a Macy's department store. She stopped to look through her purse for a piece of gum. Her lipstick and eyeliner fell to the floor. She quickly bent down to retrieve the cosmetics as did Paul, his actions mirroring hers. They almost bumped heads kneeling there, their hands outstretched for the fallen cosmetics.

Marian looked up, saw that Paul was staring into her eyes and for some damn reason she was frozen. Even when she saw him slowly leaning forward as if moving to kiss her, Marian could not bring herself to turn away. There in the middle of the fairly empty department store, Marian's personal assistant pressed his lips to hers. She did not pull back outraged and slap his face like she knew she should've, but couldn't help noticing how soft and sweet his lips were. She painfully savored them for three seconds—maybe five—before she finally reared back, swung an open hand and slapped Paul so hard her palm ached the entire, silent drive home.

After he carried the shopping bags into the house, Paul stood straight in front of Marian, his hands clasped behind his back, his eyes turned downward, like a child about to be punished.

Marian could hardly look at him. "There's no need to discuss what happened in the store because you know how wrong that was, and you know nothing like that can ever happen again."

"Yeah, I know," Paul nodded, looking up, over her shoulder past her.

"Do you really?" Marian said, wondering why she wasn't firing his ass that moment. "Dammit!"

"Yes, really," Paul said, still not looking at Marian.

"Come back tomorrow morning at 9:30. I have an appointment at 10."

The next morning Paul arrived in the clothes Marian had imagined he was most comfortable: sagging jeans, boots and a t-shirt. Without explanation he handed Marian his resignation.

"Why are you giving this to me? My husband hired you."

"I work for you."

Marian stared down at the single sentence on the dog-eared page.

I, Paul Baker, formally resign from the position of personal assistant to
Marian Lakes.

"And by the way, I'm sorry," Paul said. "I never said I was
sorry."

Marian looked up. "Why did you do it? I'm a married woman.
We were in the middle of the store. Do you know who could've seen
that?"

"You don't seem happy or fulfilled."

"You're wrong."

"I know that now."

"That can never ever happen again, do you understand?"

"Yes."

Marian crumpled the page in her hand. "Go home. Change out of
whatever it is you're wearing, and be back here in twenty minutes, or
you *will* be fired."

Now, in Neiman Marcus, Marian addressed the question of what
occasion she was buying her dress for?

"I'm buying this for mine and Larry's tenth anniversary
celebration tonight," Marian said, walking the dress over to the register
to purchase. Paul followed a step behind.

"That's nice. Where's your husband taking you?"

"Don't know yet." Marian smiled. "He's hasn't mentioned
anything, which makes me think he has something really big planned."

7

Larry knew three of the four men that sat around him in the back room of the small, rundown Auburn soul food restaurant. Bishop John Higgins sat in front of him. He was a big man who wore a lavender three-piece suit. He pulled the nub of a smoldering cigar from his lips and tapped the ashes in a nearby tray. He rubbed his huge belly and said, "I just don't think it's a good idea to continue trying to build it."

Pastor Anthony Jackson who was thin, bespectacled, and wore a suit as well, said, "I think I have to agree with the good Bishop."

"I'm not *trying* to build it," Larry said. "It's being built."

None of the men ate. All of them except one sipped from glasses of dark liquor. It was well into the evening, nearing 8 p.m., and they had been conducting this meeting in the back room with old wooden walls and floors, well-worn leather chairs and sofas, for more than forty-five minutes.

"I drive by that eyesore three or four times a week on the way to my church and haven't seen any work being done on it in a month. I don't think it's still being built Larry, and I thank God for that," Bishop Simon Ridgeway said.

Bishop Ridgeway was once Larry's spiritual father. He ran the Mount Zion Baptist church, the church Marian had first taken him to, the church where Larry was tapped on the shoulder by the Lord and told to preach—the church Larry left to start his own. Bishop Ridgeway was the man that ordained Larry, so now, as Larry took a drink of his bourbon, he wondered why Ridgeway was the man doing the most to stop him from succeeding.

"Thank God?" Larry said. "Is He the one stalling the process or is it you?"

Bishop Ridgeway was sixty-one. His head was clean-shaven, and he wore a pencil mustache. He gulped from his glass of alcohol and said, "If you're trying to accuse me of something, just say it."

Larry frowned. "The Union City mayor comes to me all of a sudden talking about some new zoning ordinances that prevent me going ahead with the build of my church. I spoke to him on many occasions during the planning of this build, and never once did he mention—"

"Maybe he didn't know then," Ridgeway said with a smile.

"Or maybe you hadn't gotten to him," Larry said.

"Gotten to him?" Ridgeway said. "What? This ain't no spy novel, boy. Maybe there are ordinances and maybe he now realizes your new church might be bad for Union City."

Larry turned away from Bishop Ridgeway. When he left the man's church to start his own, he had three hundred members in his flock. Now Larry led a congregation of over thirty thousand, almost doubling the size of Ridgeway's. Larry knew the man was mad and jealous. Ridgeway could deal with Larry running his church in the city of Atlanta, but venturing out twenty-five minutes into Union City, Georgia, Larry believed, was against Bishop Simon Ridgeway's rules.

Larry turned to Bishop John Higgins and Pastor Anthony Jackson who also had large Baptist churches in Union City, with congregations of ten and twelve thousand members respectively. "You two against me, as well?"

"I don't know what you talking about, Bishop," Bishop Higgins said, pushing his cigar back into his mouth.

30

Pastor Jackson sat up in his chair and said, "What is it about Union City? Your church is doing fine in Atlanta. Why do you need a new one?"

"Every Sunday our two overflow rooms are packed. I need more space," Larry said.

"Rumor is, attendance at Holy Sweet Spirit ain't what it used to be. And will your people even trek all the way out here?" Pastor Jackson asked.

"It's twenty-five minutes," Larry answered, ignoring Jackson's petty comment. "My people would drive an additional hour to hear me preach. But what does that have to do with—"

Bishop Higgins yanked the cigar nub from his teeth and shot a stern look at Pastor Jackson. "Just tell the man how we feel."

"You are not good for the Georgia Baptist Churches," Bishop Simon Ridgeway said.

"What did you just say?" Larry said, only now feeling as though he was being ganged up on.

The double curtain door of the room parted and an older, heavyset woman with dark skin and gray hair shuffled in wearing an apron. The men went silent.

"You men okay in here?" Earline, the owner of the establishment said.

Larry eyed the men sitting across from him. They silently, menacingly eyed him back.

"We're all fine, Mrs. Earline, and thank you so much for your wonderful hospitality," the fourth man said, standing. He was younger, Larry guessed in his mid-thirties at the oldest. Larry didn't know what reason he had to be there but figured he had some affiliation with some

31

church somewhere. He walked over to Mrs. Earline, guided her back toward the curtained door and saw her out.

"Thank you, Pastor Williams," Bishop Higgins said from within a cloud of smoke.

The young pastor Williams avoided Larry's stare and sat back down in the corner of the room.

"Like I was saying, Bishop Ridgeway continued, "Some of the things you say, the views you hold, the way you conduct yourself out there."

"What have I done?" Larry asked.

"An anti-gay march," Pastor Jackson said. "Bishop Lakes, what were you thinking?"

"It was not anti-gay. It was pro-traditional marriage, and all of you feel exactly the same way I do about that. The bible says—"

"Don't begin to tell us what the bible says," Bishop Ridgeway said. "I was interpreting the good book when you were still learning your ABC's and 123's. But when you came to each of us and asked if we wanted to take part, we told you no, that there would be significant blowback, yet you did it anyway, and you see what is happening."

"What Bishop is trying to say," Bishop Higgins said, standing from his chair, straightening the jacket of his lavender suit. "We don't want your game playing, politicking and self-promoting in Union City. Do whatever you want in Atlanta. We can't stop you no matter how much we want to, but we ain't just gonna let you tiptoe into our backyard and do whatever you please."

Larry looked up and realized all three men were standing. He rose from his chair as if to prepare for a fight. "So it's all of you that's stopping my church from going ahead?"

"We aren't admitting to that, but see it how you like," Pastor Jackson said.

Larry nodded, even smiled a little as he wagged a finger at the men surrounding him. "You're making a mistake, all of you. And young man," Larry said to Pastor Williams still seated in the corner. "Whoever you are. Don't let these men steer you into a brick wall. That's where they're headed, deceiving me like this. That church will get built and until then, I will remind you," Larry said, turning toward the exit. "Fret not thyself because of evildoers, neither be thou envious against the workers of iniquity. For they shall soon be cut down like the grass, and wither as the green herb."

8

The music in the tight, smoke-filled bar was deafening. The narrow L-shaped room teemed with people, pushing, shoving, laughing, cursing, shouting and spilling drinks as they danced at their tables.

Van Meyers, twenty-one years old, sat hunched on a stool, elbows on the bar, trying to stop himself from turning and punching the next fool that brushed passed him.

The bartender, a thin white girl with a nose ring and hair half dyed blonde/ half pink, set another glass of gin and juice in front of Van.

"Compliments from down the bar."

The glass separated into three, then morphed back into one. Van wobbled on his stool, turned to the left, looked down the crowded bar and saw a smiling, drunken face and a hand waving at him. He turned back to the drink, raised it to his face. It was the third or forth bought for him from the same person tonight.

Van's head spun, his limbs felt numb, but he would down this drink, ply himself with the poison, hoping to blot out the images and kill the nagging desire in him.

The bar stool beside him became vacant as Van tilted the glass up and started to drink. The gin was bitter, the juice sweet, and he thought he was going to vomit, but he held it down. He felt a presence beside him; someone had quickly grabbed the vacant bar stool.

"How is it, handsome?" a voice said from his left. "My name is Cashmere."

Van turned to see a brown-faced young man with big eyes colored with blue contact lenses. His hair was black, shoulder length, chemically straightened, parted down the middle and flipped up at the ends.

"Cashmere, yeah okay," Van said. He had no idea who this boy was, but he hated every fiber of him. He hated him for buying him those drinks, hated him for thinking that Van would accept the drinks, hated him for believing Van was the type that he could approach and speak to as though he knew him.

"You fine as hell Daddy," Cashmere said. "I love the yellow boys."

Van felt a hand on his thigh slowly inching toward his crotch. He didn't jump. He had the first time he felt that similar touch, but was taught not to—told that it was no reason for alarm.

Van looked sadly up, stared at his fair-complexioned face hatefully in the mirror behind the bottles of liquor. In that reflection he saw Cashmere scoot his bar stool closer, bring his mouth very close to the side of Van's face. Van clenched his teeth as he felt Cashmere's warm breath enter his ear.

"I wonder if this dick is as golden as the rest of you."

Cashmere squeezed Van's penis. Van cursed his erection, hated that he had become this person, that he had not yet found a way to turn himself back into the boy he was.

"Can I find out?" Cashmere asked.

Van lifted his drink, guzzled what remained and slammed the glass down. "Fuck it," Van said. "Whatever."

Inside the bathroom stall, Van fell onto the toilet and watched through blurry eyes as Cashmere turned and locked the stall door.

Van's head spun as he heard someone outside washing their hands at the sink, then someone flushing a toilet in the stall next door. He looked down, saw Cashmere deftly unfastening his belt and his jeans. Van's erect penis was bared, and Cashmere with those big, baby-doll-blue eyes, looked up at him smiling.

"Mmm, I'm gonna love this." He wrapped his hand around Van with fingers Van just noticed were painted pink then took him all the way into his mouth. This was supposed to feel good, but in Van's mind Cashmere's saliva felt like acid and the occasional scrape of his teeth felt like the ends of broken bottles. Inside his head, Van screamed in agony as he watched Cashmere's head bob up and down, Van's body starting to give.

Cashmere moaned in approval, stroking and sucking faster, urging Van to the point of release.

Van groaned, squirmed and fought the boy's efforts to make him succumb. A tear spilled from his eye as he grabbed a fistful of Cashmere's hair and tore him off.

"Baby, baby, it's cool," Cashmere said, his hair all about his head, his lips, chin and cheeks shiny with saliva. "You can come in my mouth."

"No. No! This is not me," Van said, the screaming in his head so loud now he wasn't able to hear himself speak.

Cashmere laughed. "Yeah, right." He reached for Van's penis again. "Give me that dick."

Van knocked Cashmere's hand away, drunkenly stood from the toilet seat and pulled up his pants.

"What...I ain't finished, boy," Cashmere said, grabbing onto Van's belt.

Van shoved Cashmere against the stall door, shoved his forearm into his throat. "Just let me walk out of here and I promise I won't hurt you," Van said, more tears wetting his face, his right fist raised just above his shoulder. "If you don't, I swear I'll hurt you."

Wriggling out from under Van's hold, Cashmere said, "Gone, boy." He stepped out the way of the door and said, "Your dick wasn't all that good no way."

9

Marian sat half drunk at the kitchen table. The room was dark save for a candle that flickered, casting long shadows against the walls. The kids had been put to bed almost two hours ago, and Marian's mother had kissed her, wished her daughter goodnight and a wonderful time celebrating her anniversary.

"I know I'm not always nice to the man," Estelle said, smiling. "But he does what he's supposed to do as a father and husband, so I can't be too mad at him."

Marian thought to, but didn't tell her mother that Larry did what he had to do most of the time, but in the bedroom, he had been falling off pretty badly.

"But if he ever slips up," Estelle said, turning back, about to ascend the first step leading upstairs. "I'll be on his ass."

"You know I know that, Mommy."

An hour and a half before taking the seat at the kitchen table, Marian had showered, did her makeup and hair and slid into the dress she had bought earlier. It had fit just the way she had imagined, and with her diamond earrings, bracelet and the necklace Larry had given her for their last anniversary, she believed her husband would think her gorgeous. He would take her out on the town so they could do whatever he had planned for them, and when they returned home, her husband would be so turned on that he could not keep his hands off of her. That wasn't something that Marian just dreamt of, it was something that had to happen.

Over the last year, she felt Larry treated her like nothing more than a disturbance—one more situation to manage in the course of his busy day, pushing time with her and the family aside for duties of the church.

When they were alone, in their bedroom, he would not show Marian the affection she was accustomed to from the years when they were first married. Many nights, she'd lie in bed—on the nights he was even there—and stare up at the ceiling after Larry told her he was tired, and he would make it up to her.

He had told her that again just last week, and not once since had he reached across the bed, slid a hand under her nightgown or lay his lips upon her face long enough to be considered more than a friendly peck.

The last time she felt her husband inside of her was more than three months ago.

Was this how she was supposed to be living? Marian asked herself, pouring more of the champagne into her flute—the champagne she had set out on the table to toast their special night.

Her shoes kicked off, her stocking feet crossed in one of the kitchen chairs, Marian had drank more than half the bottle. She had long ago felt the effects of the alcohol and again she questioned if, and for how long she was to tolerate this neglect.

She leaned forward to grab her cell phone and almost fell out of her chair she was so intoxicated. The tiny illuminated numbers were blurry, but she managed to dial her husband. She knew he hated when she called out for him, but she believed in this case the call was warranted.

The phone was picked up on the first ring.

"What are you doing? When are you coming home?" Marian asked.

"I'll be home shortly, but didn't I tell you about doing this? If I'm not there, it's because I'm busy doing something that's important enough to keep me away, important enough to not be interrupted. Right?"

"Yes, that's right," Marian said, realizing by the sound of her husband's voice that he had no clue he had forgotten their tenth anniversary.

She was crushed and thought to tell him he missed it but decided she'd enjoy the misery he'd suffer when he found out on his own.

"Then I'll see you when I get home, and don't wait up. Okay?" Larry said.

"Yeah okay, Larry," Marian said. She set the phone down, picked up the bottle beside her and filled her glass till champagne spilled over the rim.

"Who was that, your wife?" Shreeva asked.

Larry slipped the phone back into the pocket of his suit jacket. "You know who it was."

"I know, Daddy," Shreeva purred, pressing a hand with freshly manicured, bright pink fingernails to Larry's chest. Shreeva lay across her comforter wearing nothing but a sheer pink teddy. For thirty-six years old, her body was incredible. Her light brown skin was flawless, her eyes alluring, her lips big, soft and succulent, daring a man to think of anything else but a sloppy, wet blowjob when looking at them. She had the shape of a collegiate track star—narrow waist, thick thighs, big calves and breasts that had men shamefully gawking from across rooms. She wore her hair shoulder length and perfectly styled. A single black dot of a beauty mark sat just above the left corner of her mouth.

Shreeva fussed with one of the buttons on Larry's shirt, trying to undo it. "I just wanna know when you gonna divorce her and marry me?"

Larry sighed to himself, wondering if maintaining this side relationship was still beneficial to him.

He had known Shreeva for more than fifteen years—five years longer than he'd known his wife.

Shreeva loved Larry hard, was the perfect woman for him back when he was younger, still hustling. She had his back, would enthusiastically take a bullet or put one in a man to save his life. He thought at first that was all he needed and promised to marry her after he became successful. But after five years of struggle and no sign of things improving for him, Larry realized he would need help. Shreeva was beautiful and more devoted than any woman he had ever been with, but she lived check to check, as was he. If Larry were ever to fulfill the promise he made to himself of never again feeling the pain of poverty, he knew he would have to align himself with a woman of means.

The night after meeting Marian, Larry sat at a card table and watched his friend Tyrell Suggs spread marijuana leaves into brown cigar paper. He sealed the cigar with a lick of his tongue then passed it to Larry.

Larry hesitated then took the blunt. "This gonna have to be my last one."

"Cool," Tyrell said. "We can smoke this one, and I'll roll another later on."

"Naw, my last one ever. I met a girl—a good one. She been to school, come from a good family with money, the type of girl a man could build himself up with. I told you I can't be broke, living hand to mouth all my life. I did that as a boy. Ain't trying to do it too much longer as a man."

"What about Shreeva? You tell her about this good girl?" Tyrell Suggs said, holding the cigarette lighter out to Larry.

Larry lit the blunt, brought it to his lips, pulled some smoke into his lungs and winced slightly. I love Shreeva. That woman will do anything for me. Girls like that are hard to come by. I don't want to lose her, but I'll tell her. She can stay on if she wants, but that'll have to be with the knowledge that she ain't first no more."

Tyrell Suggs took the blunt that Larry passed him. "Not sure if that's gonna happen, knowing Shreeva."

"Guess we won't know till I tell her."

The next night, Larry stood in the bedroom of Shreeva's one bedroom apartment. She sat on the edge of her bed wearing a faded pink nightgown, one strap falling off her shoulder, her face in her hands, bawling.

Larry had just given her the news; he had met another woman and he wanted to pursue something with her.

"Shreeva," Larry said. "Stop crying, baby."

Shreeva looked up. Tears blackened by mascara crawled down her cheeks. "Stop crying? What am I supposed to do? You told me you would marry me. You told me we'd be together, and now you leaving me?" She stood, pointed a finger in Larry's face. "All I've been is devoted to you, and you do this! Look at this shithole I live in. How am I supposed to make it without you?"

Larry looked around the tiny apartment, and only after spending time in the four bedroom house that Marian owned, did this place look as small and disgusting as Shreeva called it. Over the five years they had been together, Larry gave Shreeva money when she asked, paid her rent when she needed him to, had been the support she couldn't have lived without. He didn't know if she was more distraught about losing him, or losing what he provided.

"You know I love you." It was the only thing Larry could think to say. "I love you, and I want you to still be able to make it. You can stay if you want. I can still help you out. Won't a whole lot change if you wanna stay with me."

Shreeva smoothed the tears from her face, sniffled. "Really, Larry?" she said, sarcasm in her voice. "You want me to stay as you fuck some other bitch? Want me to stay, act as your mistress when I was supposed to be your wife?" Shreeva walked toward her dresser. She stood in the mirror, her face down, sobbing. Suddenly, she turned, slung a heavy wooden hairbrush at Larry. It struck him on the cheek, just under his right eye. He covered his face, dropped to his knees in awful pain.

He blinked several times and opened his eyes to see Shreeva's bare feet just in front of him. He lifted his head, looking at Shreeva through his one good eye.

"Okay Larry," Shreeva said, sadly. "I'll be your mistress. Whatever you want."

Since then it seemed every time Larry saw Shreeva, he dealt with the question of when he would leave his wife and marry her.

"I told you," Larry said now, grabbing Shreeva's wrist and setting her hand on her bare thigh. "In due time. When the time is right."

"When the new church is finished, right? I'm gonna be your new first lady," Shreeva reminded him of the promise he made when he decided he would build a new spiritual home a little over a year ago. He made her that promise because she demanded it of him. Without that assurance, she threatened to leave. Larry lived so long with Shreeva in life, he couldn't imagine what it would be like without her.

"That's right, but till then, you gotta be patient." Larry stood from the king sized bed that sat in the middle of the huge bedroom. Windows constructed three quarters of the space, giving a beautiful view of Atlanta's downtown skyline at night. He dug in his slacks pocket, pulled out a business size envelope filled with the cash that would pay the mortgage on the swank, 2,500 square foot condo and the note on the red Infiniti G37 Shreeva sped through town in everyday.

"Thank you, Daddy. You know how much you mean to me, right?"

44

Larry knew, but she meant a great deal to him as well. This was where he came when he did not want to go home, when being a father and husband, along with bishop of the largest Baptist church in the south became too much. He had helped Shreeva when they were both poor, and he would not abandon her now that he was well off.

Larry grabbed his jacket from off the back of a purple, velvet-covered chair and slipped into it.

Shreeva sat up on her knees in bed and curled a finger at him.

"What can I do for you?"

"Why don't you hook me up with a quickie till I see you again," Shreeva said. "It's been such a long time since I've felt you."

"I'm sure you haven't been going without," Larry said, glancing over the room for signs of the men he knew visited her.

"I only do it because I can't have you, and you said it was okay. You know that don't you, baby?"

Larry glanced down at his watch, a gold Cartier Roadster XL. "It's already after 11. I gotta get back."

"Then let me give you something to take with you," Shreeva said, attempting to unzip his trousers.

Larry caught her hand before she could reach in his pants and pull him out. He leaned over and softly kissed her knuckle. "That's not necessary. You have a good night."

11

It was twenty minutes till midnight, and Van stood in the poorly lit hallway of an old apartment building. The carpet underfoot was soiled and worn; the paint on the walls was chipped and marked with vulgar graffiti. Van hung his head low, pushed open the door of his studio apartment. The sound of his one-year-old baby crying assaulted his ears.

"Where have you been?" Sierra, his wife of nine months yelled. She wore a gray and black security guard uniform. She bounced their son, Virgil, on her hip. Sierra was thin, twenty-two years-old, but didn't look a day over sixteen with her blemish-free skin, bright, big eyes and light brown hair pulled back in a pig tail. Virgil looked more like his mother than Van. The baby had her brown skin, tiny nose, wide eyes, and a head full of curly hair.

"I said where you been, Van? You know I gotta be at work in twenty minutes," Sierra said, holding Virgil by his armpits out for Van to take. The baby was naked save for his diaper. He screamed, holding out his arms to his father.

Van pressed Virgil close to his chest, bounced him a little, trying to quiet his screams. "Baby, I'm sorry. But I'm back for you to get to work in time."

Sierra looked at Van with disappointment, shaking her head. "Dammit, Van, you're going to have to tell me what's going on with you. Your head always somewhere else. We can't keep on like this."

"Baby, ain't nothing going on with me."

"Whatever," Sierra said, walking to him. She kissed him on the lips and the baby on his head. "He's already been fed and changed. Don't

46

know why the hell he's crying. And that was the last of his food. Hope you got money for some more."

No, Van didn't. He paid the last money he had on the electric bill, and wouldn't be paid till next week. "Yeah, okay."

"It ain't much, but your dinner is sitting in the microwave. I gotta go."

Sierra stepped out and left Van holding the baby and the door. He watched his wife till she turned the corner and heard her descending the creaking stairs.

Van pushed the door closed with a kick of his foot, quickly set his now quiet son back in his crib, where he started to cry again.

"Shut up," Van said, softly, not to the boy, but to the thoughts in his head—the image of the boy in the club going down on him, stroking him, trying to get him to—

"No," Van said, pressing a hand against the counter as though he feared he would fall. He asked himself why he was still suffering like this.

After he was put out of the church, after he was sent away, he was directionless and depressed. Sierra, then his girlfriend of three years, asked him what was wrong. Could she do anything to help him? They were sitting across from each other in a McDonald's on Martin Luther King Drive, sharing a cheeseburger and small fries when she had asked him that.

If she only knew the sense of betrayal and loneliness he felt at that moment. Van stared in her eyes. She'd always been there for him, always comforted him after the times he had been humiliated and taken by that man, even though Van never told her about those encounters. She rubbed his head, held him close, promised that she'd be there whenever he was ready to tell her what was truly bothering him.

"Will you marry me?" Van said in that McDonald's, feeling helpless, feeling there was nothing left to live for. "I don't have no ring or anything, but will you just marry me?" He assumed Sierra didn't hear the desperation in his voice because she smiled, jumped out of the booth, came around his side, threw her arms around him and said, "Yes, baby! I'll marry you!"

He made her an honest woman under God, him an honest man— thought life would've been perfect after that or at least improve a little, but still the thoughts, the shame and the regret still tormented him.

Van turned toward his son. Virgil was standing in the crib, wailing, his face wet and pink, looking as though he was in agony. Was he? Was he being tortured like his father, wondering if he could take another day, wondering if he was better off dead?

Leaning against the counter, still fighting the images from earlier that night that tried to enter his head, Van knew what had to be done. He pushed himself up, walked purposely across the apartment to the closet. He snatched open the door, reached all the way back on the overhead shelf and pulled out a handgun. He sat on the mattress of the let-out bed, staring at the gun in his hand.

His son still screamed, but the noise seemed muted now. Van felt alone in the room, trying to convince himself that what he was thinking was not the best answer to his problems. If this didn't happen, he feared he would keep on with the bars and the boys till Sierra found out. He raised the gun, pressed the barrel to his temple and started to squeeze the trigger, but paused when he caught sight of his son. The boy had stopped crying again, his eyes open wide, a strange look of understanding in them as if he knew exactly what was going on.

Van couldn't do this in front of the boy. He brought the gun down, and rose from the mattress. He would take his child with him and save him from possibly turning into what his father was, from experiencing the hell he was going through.

Van stepped in front of the crib, lifted the gun and pointed it at his son. Virgil, leaning against the rail, started to cry again. Van moved the gun closer, an inch from the boy's forehead.

Virgil cried even louder, reached out a chubby hand, tried pushing the barrel of the gun away as he looked into his father's eyes as if to ask why he was doing this.

Van answered aloud, "This will be better for the both of us." It'll be quick he told himself. Van tightened his finger against the trigger, pulling back on it when a knock came at the door.

He whipped his head in that direction, ignored the disturbance, then refocused his attention on the task at hand. Again he made the effort to free him and his son when the pounding at the door came louder. "Van, it's me."

Van forced the gun down, shutting his eyes, wanting to cry. "Fuck!" he said, softly. He looked at Virgil. The boy looked back as if to ask, what now?

Van hurried across the room, set the gun under his pillow on the let-out sofa bed.

When he pulled open the door, his friend Urail stood behind it, wearing a beaten winter coat, fur around the hood, and rain boots. The clothes he wore were filthy. His hair was long and uncombed and long facial hair spotted his cheeks and chin.

"I waited till after your girl gone to work. I know she don't like me," Urail said, stepping in without being invited. "I know she don't like me."

"What are you doing here?"

"It's raining outside. Can I sleep here tonight? I don't like to get wet, and it's raining." Urail walked directly to the same corner of the room where Van had allowed him to sleep countless other nights when the weather was bad. Urail pulled his hood over his head, lay down on his back and crossed his arms over his chest.

"Yeah, you can sleep here tonight, man." Van walked over to his son who had stopped crying, and by the look of wonder on his face, seemed somewhat entertained by the man who had walked in. Van lifted the boy and lay him down on his back. He then walked over to the let-out bed, kicked off his shoes and slid under the blankets fully clothed. He pulled the gun from under the pillow and set it under the bed then clicked off the bedside lamp.

The room was pitch black, but Van's eyes were wide open. He knew he would have trouble finding sleep tonight. He rolled on his side.

"Van, you ever think about him?" Urail asked from the corner in the dark.

"No."

"You ever think about why he did that to us?"

"No, Urail. Just go to sleep, man."

"I been thinking a lot about it, and I'm gonna do something about it."

Van lay on his back again, lightly pounded his forehead with the flat of his fist,

50

wishing Urail would shut up. "Fine. Do whatever you want, but just go to sleep."

"Okay, Van."

12

In bed, Marian heard the mechanical movement of the garage door when it rolled up. She heard the Bentley pull in, the doors slam, and then after a few moments, the engine of Tyrell Suggs's new Monte Carlo come to life as he prepared to drive home after a long day of chauffeuring around her husband.

Tipsy, but more sick from drinking the entire bottle of champagne, Marian stumbled upstairs and found herself on her knees, bent over the toilet, with her beautiful newly bought dress hiked up while she vomited up her insides. The dress was now thrown over a chair on the other side of the bedroom.

Marian had managed to doze off a little over an hour ago, but she lay awake now.

She rolled over, caught sight of the glowing red numbers on the alarm clock—11:22 p.m. She closed her eyes. She heard the sound of feet outside the door. It opened. Larry tipped about the room in the dark, undressing, laying his clothes on the bench in front of the bed, then carefully, eased under the linen with Marian.

She felt his body relax beside her. She thought of trying to get back to sleep, let him be, but she thought that maybe there was the slightest chance that he would realize before the day got away from him entirely, that he could still wish her Happy Anniversary. She opened her eyes, checked the clock again. He had 37 minutes left.

"Larry," Marian said.

"Yeah," Larry answered as if not surprised she was awake.

"You have a good day?"

"There was good and there was bad, but God has gotten me through it."

"Amen," Marian said.

"There are issues with the building of the new church. We're losing lots of money with it just sitting there nearly finished. If that's not bad enough, the congregation is not giving like they used to. It's not a good situation."

Marian heard him sigh heavily.

"I'm thinking about…no, I'm going to ask the congregation to give more tomorrow at Sunday service."

Marian was angry with her husband, but it was still her responsibility to give him input when she believed he was about to make a mistake. "I know the economy is getting better, but times are still tight for most everybody. Those people come to our church looking for hope to help them deal with *not* having money, and you're going to ask them for more. They're hurting and—with all due respect, Larry, I don't think that's the right thing to do. Those people are struggling, and—"

"And we aren't?" Larry said, anger all of a sudden in his voice. "When they are down, when they are troubled, when they seek answers, who do they come to, and who gives without question?"

"We do, but—"

"They are not the only ones in need, Marian. You may not know this, but our family is hurting too. Do you want our children to go without? Do you want us to live in poverty?"

"Larry, I know you have painful memories from when you were a child living that way, but our children will never experience—"

Marian heard her husband quickly shuffling around in bed. His bedside
lamp came on, filling the room with light, causing her to squint.

"How do you know our children will never experience that?" Larry said, his face contorted into a mask of worry. "What if something happens to me? What if something brings down our church?"

"Like what?" Marian asked.

"I don't know, what if someone tries to smear my name? What if they succeed?"
He sat up. "I don't care what you say, tomorrow our members best be prepared to dig a little deeper," Larry said, his arms crossed over his chest, his eyes staring out over the large bedroom.

Marian watched him, telling herself this was not the first time he hadn't listened to a word of advice she gave him. It wouldn't be the last. She was about to roll back over, but noticed Larry caught sight of her black dress thrown sloppily over the chair, the black heels on the carpet beneath it. He turned to her.

"Did you go—"He stopped himself, his mouth open as if to ask another question, but instead, he shut his eyes appearing pained by something. He opened them, grabbed Marian's hand and squeezed it. "I…I…I'm so, so sorry I forgot our anniversary, didn't I? Why didn't you tell me?"

"Should I have to? The past few years, I didn't have to because…never mind," Marian said, feeling as though she would cry. "Do I really have to remind you of our anniversary?"

"No, I guess not. I was just so caught up in—"

"I know, Larry. You told me."

"I'll make it up to you. I will. I promise."

Marian eased her hand from her husband's grasp and pulled the blanket up before saying, "Don't worry about it. We didn't celebrate our anniversary, but we celebrate our wonderful marriage every day, right?"

"That's right," Larry said.

Marian pulled up her side of the blanket, but before rolling over, she said, "My girlfriend knows a marriage counselor. I'm going to make an appointment for us. I think we could benefit from talking to someone. Will you go?"

Larry took a moment to answer. He looked insulted and disappointed that she would ask such a thing of him.

"Yeah Marian, I'll go."

13

The next morning, Robby stepped into the doorway of the prison common showers with two of his co-workers. Officer Gerald and Officer Oaks stood on either side of him, their service clubs in their hands.

Thick steam filled the large room with floors and walls covered with tile. A dozen showerheads were spaced equally apart—half of them running, spitting out hot water as six naked inmates washed under them. One of those men was Rasheed Jenkins. Of the men who raped Treyshaun, Rasheed was the only one Treyshaun could finger with certainty.

Robby knew Gerald and Oaks hated men like Jenkins as much as he did. Gerald's sister was attacked and raped when she was sixteen years old. Mentally scarred, Gerald said she had never been the same since. Oaks's mother was beaten and raped not two years ago. They found her in a vacant lot, barely breathing in a vacant lot. Oaks by her side, she later died in the hospital from her wounds. It took the two men not ten seconds to agree to teach Rasheed Jenkins a lesson once Robby told them what the inmate had done.

Glancing through the steam, one of the showering inmates saw the dark forms of Robby and the other officers. He set his bar of soap in the holder, tapped the man next to him and they silently retreated from the room. Three other inmates smartly followed, walking past Robby, their heads down, their towels and other belongings in hand, as if clueless of what was about to happen.

Rahseed continued to soap and wash his face, oblivious to the fact that he was alone.

Robby stared at the muscular naked man and fought the memories that tried to yank him back to when he was just a powerless teen, standing in a hotel shower, afraid to deny the man standing naked, holding his raging erection, in front of him.

Robby cringed, shut his eyes to blank the memory from his brain.

"Jenkins!" Robby's voice echoed through the room over the crash of running water. Startled, Rasheed Jenkins rinsed the soap from his face. He turned around squinting, surprised to see that he was by himself.

"What the fuck's going on?" Jenkins said, reaching to his side, turning the water off.

Robby stepped forward, hating Jenkins even though he hadn't known of the man before just the other day. "You like fucking dudes up the ass, yo?"

"What did you say?" Jenkins said, taking a barefoot step forward as if planning to take on the three officers by himself.

"You heard what I motherfucking said. Like taking man-ass much without permission?"

"I don't know what the fuck you talkin 'bout, man."

Robby saw that Gerald and Oaks had turned off the other showers and had already surrounded Jenkins, waiting for permission to pounce.

"Wrong answer, playa," Robby said. "You here cause you paying for breaking the law outside. Now you broke the law inside. You fucked up, dude."

Robby turned to see that Gerald and Oaks had started advancing on Jenkins. The inmate swung on the officers in wide sweeping arcs, but

Gerald chopped him at the shin with his club, bringing Jenkins to the wet shower floor. There the two men swung their clubs heavily down on Jenkins as he squirmed, writhed, cursed and yelled, attempting to shield himself with his arms and legs. Blood flowed from Jenkins's wounds into the water, across the tile floor and down the shower drains. Oaks raised his club high over his head, brought it down on Jenkins's leg, snapping it. The inmate screamed and reached down toward his broken bone. Gerald and Oaks wrestled him into submission, one on either side of him, each holding an arm and a leg, the man's ass hiked up.

"You wanna take some ass! You the big man that wanna hold somebody down and rape them!" Oaks yelled while Robby stood, clutching his club in his sweat-drenched fist, only now wondering if this was the right course of action to have taken.

"Gentry! Bring your club over here!" Gerald yelled to Robby.

"We gonna show you what that feels like, nigga!" Gerald said to Jenkins.

"Gentry, grab your club and shove it up this motherfucker's ass!"

Robby hurried forward, stood behind Jenkins.

"Do it!" Oaks said.

Robby raised his club, prepared to force the end of it into Jenkins's anus, make him familiar with the excruciating pain he caused Treyshaun.

"Do it!" Both officers yelled, still struggling to restrain Jenkins.

But Robby was stolen away to when he was sixteen, standing in front of that man embarrassed and afraid. It was just the day after Bishop entered him for the first time. And as instructed, Robby had not told his mother. He had not gone to the police. He hadn't told a soul, not even his best friends Van and Urail.

58

"When…when I sat down to go, I was bleeding from back there," Robby told Bishop the day after they first had sex.

Bishop smiled, placed a hand to Robby's cheek. "It's nothing to worry about. It's natural. It'll go away soon enough."

"Gentry! Goddammit!" Robby heard Oaks' yell echo through the shower room, snapping him out of thoughts. "Take your stick and—"

"No! Let him go!" Robby said, changing his mind.

"What?"

"I said let him go!" Robby stooped to look Jenkins in the eyes. They were barely open. His cheek lay on the wet tile. He appeared close to losing consciousness. "You broke his leg and he's fucked up enough. Let him go!"

"What the fuck are you talking about?" Oaks said.

"You fucking sure?" Gerald said.

"Just let him go!" Robby said. "I'm sure."

Gerald glanced at Oaks. Both men shook their heads then released Jenkins. Robby grabbed a clump of the thick, uncombed hair atop Jenkins's skull and wrenched his head up so that their eyes met.

"You or any motherfucking body you know rape anyone in this jail again, I promise, I won't be here to stop what these men will do to you next time."

14

Sunday morning Larry had something to preach about. As he stepped out on the stage wearing his bishop's gown, he gazed over the thousands of black faces, his loyal followers filling every single seat of the huge church's beautiful sanctuary. This moment always gave him pause, always took his breath away and reminded him how grateful he should be that God touched him on the shoulder that one fateful Sunday.

Ten years ago, having no job after being fired from the used car dealership, Larry was down on himself. He knew he wanted to be more, do more than just sell cars. Marian, his girlfriend of six months supported him financially. She didn't urge him to find work, but pushed him to attend church with her, "To find God", she said, which might help him discover what he wanted to do for the rest of his life.

Larry had never gone to church—never wanted to, but to appease the woman, he accompanied her to the Mount Zion Baptist Church.

He was not moved by the spirit and had found no new desire to be saved, but what Larry did do was sit in awe of the man preaching. Larry marveled at the control he had over the audience, the use he made of his voice, his gestures: the sweeping arm movements, the stomping and dancing across stage and the patting of his brow to dry his sweat. When the preacher, his name was Pasture Richards, spoke, the audience of nearly a thousand was deathly silent. But when Pasture Richards got excited and screamed at his congregation, demanding they become as enthusiastic, members of the church howled and hollered with him, raised their hands, shouted, danced, spoke in tongues and fainted, so overwhelmed with the message. Collection plates were passed around several times, and in appreciation of the preacher's words, his followers filled those plates to the point of spilling over with coins, dollars and even personal checks. Larry believed going to church with Marian was going to be a waste of time, but that moment, after the first service he ever attended, he turned to Marian, squeezed her hand and smiled, knowing he had accomplished what she had wanted him to. He had found God.

Larry walked toward the pulpit, receiving applause as people cried out to him. He passed the deacons of the church, respectively nodded to them. His wife sat on the other side of the pulpit. He walked over, took her hand, brought it to his lips, kissed it and told her he loved her.

There was more applause. He turned to his adoring congregation and pulled out his notes. Today's sermon had been written almost a week ago, but after the events of the last few days, he knew he could not read what had already been prepared.

Bishop Larry Lakes stepped up to the podium, rested hands on either side of it, leaned toward the audience and said, "How y'all doin, today?"

The congregation replied, most of them saying, "Fine." Some said, "Good" and "Well", but not with the energy Larry was looking for.

"I said, how y'all feelin this wonderful, blessed Sunday morning?" Larry yelled into the tiny microphone headset he wore.

The congregation responded in kind, yelling, "Fine!" and "We are blessed!"

He smiled, looking over their faces, seeing the love they had for him, the love and devotion they had for the good Lord. He left the podium, walked about the stage. Staring out into the crowd, he saw Shreeva sitting very near the front. She had never missed a Sunday morning service since he preached his first. She winked at him, pursed her lips and motioned a kiss. He nodded back to her.

"That's the energy I'm talking about," Larry said to his followers, lowering his voice just a bit. He raised the notes so everyone could see. "This was gonna be the sermon today." He folded the pages and slid them into his shirt pocket. "But there have been some folks in the news talkin' about old Bishop Larry Lakes."

People in the pews said, "Who?" and "Talk about it."

"Y'all been hearing what they been saying about your bishop and his march, haven't y'all? They been saying that it was wrong, that Bishop Larry Lakes is anti-gay, and anti gay marriage. They say that he is politicking, trying to push his own agenda to get money given to him." Larry raised his voice even louder, yelling when he said, "That's what they been sayin! Have you heard 'em?"

The congregation, in unison, yelled, "Yeah!"

"Can you believe that?" Larry yelled.

"No!"

"I can't either, because Bishop Larry Lakes does not have to politic, pander or beg. If anyone wishes to donate to this church, than they are more than welcome to, and they shall do that on their own accord. I ain't asking them for nothing. And I ain't anti-gay, I'm just pro-marriage." Larry paused, thoughtfully. "Did you hear what I said, church?"

The church yelled, "Yeah!"

"I ain't anti-gay, I'm just pro-marriage, and believe that real, true marriage is meant to be between a man and a woman. Can I get an amen?"

"Amen!" the church said.

Larry walked silently across the stage, methodically rubbing his chin. "I don't know, y'all," he said, his voice very low now, but still loud enough for the entire church to hear him through the many speakers hanging overhead. "I don't know who they trying to make me into. I love all of God's children, but some of them have just lost their way, and part of the reason for the march was to let them know that I am offering them salvation. This church is offering a solution to their problem, a cure to what ails them, a light down that dark path they're traveling," Larry said, his voice increasing in volume and passion with each word. "I am offering them that which will make them whole, yet I am being made into a monster. I can't understand it!"

The churched cheered, many of the members where out of their chairs, waving, pumping their fists, shaking their heads.

"I think they're trying to turn my own congregation against me."

"No!" the entire church said.

"I think they are, and I think they may have swayed some of y'all."

"No!"

Larry went silent again as he walked back across the stage. He pulled a handkerchief from his back pocket, blotted the sweat from his forehead then turned to the congregation. "It's a little warm in here, ain't it?"

Members of the church fanned themselves with pamphlets and folded fast food carry out menus—anything that could create a flow of air. "Yes," they agreed.

"And kind of tight, too. I see y'all standing in the back there," Larry said, squinting, holding a hand over his eyes as if they were miles away.

Laughter was heard throughout the sanctuary.

"I been telling y'all about that big, beautiful church I've been building in Union City for y'all, right?"

"Yes," the church responded.

"Well, there are people trying to stop me from finishing it. It's just about built. It's almost there, but it sits there like some museum exhibit. You can look at it, but you can't touch it or use it, and to be quite frank…" Larry turned to glance at Marian, knowing she had objected to what he was about to do. "…we're losing a lot of money. Church, we are losing a lot of money, not just with the building of our new home, but like I said, I think the media has gotten to some of y'all because a lot of you stopped coming, and the ones who still do, a lot of y'all stopped giving."

Larry saw that his wife had lowered her face into her hand. But the church was giving him the response he had desired. The members seemed shocked, and were turning to one another as if to accuse their neighbor of cheating the church out of what it was due.

"So I'm gonna make a plea in the name of our current spiritual home, and our spiritual home to be. I'm gonna make a plea that today, when you give, you give as much as you can in order to help us through this hard time. Will you answer this plea?"

The congregation enthusiastically said, "Yes!"

Larry turned again to Marian who was staring directly at him now. He raised his voice, and said, "I said, will you answer this plea? Will you give to your embattled Bishop in this time of crisis so that he can build our beautiful new spiritual home and safely deliver us there? Will you?"

And the church said with more energy, "Yes!"

Larry smiled, lowered his voice, blotted his face again and said, "Amen."

After service, Larry walked among the congregation, as they found their way toward the exit. He spotted a woman in her middle thirties, well built, wearing a pink skirt suit and pink gloves. Larry smiled, and walked over to her.

"Ms. Lewis," Larry said, extending his hand to her. "Did you enjoy the sermon?"

Ms. Lewis gratefully took Larry's hand and shook it. "It was wonderful as always. It's a shame what the media is doing to you, and I gave extra today, so don't you worry."

"Thank you, thank you." Larry turned to the young man standing next to Ms. Lewis. He was attractive and tall, an inch or so shorter than Larry's six feet. He wore a dark suit and tie and looked to have had a fresh haircut.

"And Omar, what did you think?" Larry said, resting a hand on the seventeen-year-old boy's shoulder. The act sent a chill through Larry's body and a memory through his brain of the first young man he invited into his Boy's Ministry almost ten years ago.

Omar smiled bashfully, a dimple appearing in his left cheek. "It was good."

"You coming to the boy's ministry meeting on Wednesday?"

"Yes, Bishop," Omar said.

"Good, we look forward to seeing you."

Omar turned to his mother. "I gotta run to the rest room before we leave."

Ms. Lewis excused her son then gently took Larry by the wrist before he walked off.

"Bishop Lakes, I just want to thank you for everything you're doing with my son. Him being in your boy's ministry the last two years has really helped him, and without him having a father present—"

Larry smiled and shook his head. "No, no, no you don't. It is our pleasure to have him. Are you going to let him participate in the California trip I'm taking some of the boys on?"

Ms. Lewis appeared saddened. "That's all he's been talking about, but I just can't afford it."

Larry looked over both his shoulders then sidled up to Ms. Lewis as though to tell her a very special secret. "I tell you what, you give Omar permission to go, I'll work out a way for the church to pay for it."

Ms. Lewis jumped excitedly, threw her arms around Larry and gave him a hug. "Oh my goodness, thank you, thank you, so much!"

He stepped back, smiled again and said, "The pleasure will be all mine."

15

Marian walked about the foyer of the church, speaking to the members who approached and informed her of how much they had enjoyed her husband's message.

The majority of the congregation agreed with what Larry had to say about the media coming after him, about him and his church being the target of some conspiracy to bring them both down. Did Marian believe that? It didn't matter. What she didn't appreciate was Larry not taking a moment last night to consider what she said about asking members of the church to give more. Yes, most of them gave happily, but as Marian walked about now, she overheard bits of hushed conversations of people who did not appreciate Larry asking them to dig deeper into their wallets and pocket books to support the church.

"We got to live, too." Marian heard someone say somewhere behind her. Marian listened as a woman responded. "Do you know how much I've given this church over the last year?" Then Marian saw a woman who was cradling a newborn baby, say, "If the church hurtin' so bad, why the Lakes's still got a Bentley and a Lincoln parked around back?"

That particular woman quickly quieted herself and smiled when she saw Marian staring her in the mouth. Marian thought of going over there to the group of three women and apologizing for her husband, but that wasn't her place. She was the first lady, nothing but a figurehead position. She had no power in the church—no say. She wasn't a bishop, only the wife of one, her role being to support him, his decisions and efforts.

Marian walked into the west-side dayroom where bible classes were held and many of the children played after services. Jabari and Simone ran up to her, Simone hugging her leg, Jabari pulling on her arm.

"Can we go to McDonald's, Mommy? Please, please, please!" both children wined in unison.

"Not a chance, children. We'll make you something good at McLakes's. It's better for you, and the food is already paid for."

Jabari and Simone waved goodbye to their friends, grabbed either of their mother's hands and started out the dayroom when they bumped into their father.

"Daddy!" Simone said.

Larry bent down, hoisted his daughter up, held her in his arms and kissed her on the cheek. "How's my baby-boo?"

"Fine, daddy," Simone smiled.

"Good," Larry said, setting his daughter down and rubbing his son on the head.

Marian looked on expressionless.

"What did I tell you?" Larry said. "They listened to what I asked them and had no problem giving more."

"You don't know that," Marian snapped.

"I do know that."

"You don't even listen to me," Marian whispered harshly.

"Marian—" Larry started.

"You forget about our anniversary and—"

"Marian—"

"You come in at night when you want."

"Marian—"

"Mommy!" Simone cried. "You're hurting my hand."

Marian looked down and only then realized she was tightly squeezing both her children's hands. She glanced at Jabari. He shot her back a bewildered glare. She quickly bent down, took her daughter's hand and kissed it several times. "I'm so sorry, baby. Mommy didn't mean it. You okay?"

Simone stuck out her bottom lip. She didn't respond.

"I said are you okay?" Marian demanded a response.

The child nodded.

"Good." Marian stood, stared at her husband. He eyed her back disapprovingly.

"We can talk more about this when I get home," Larry said.

"No, it's fine. I've said all I needed to say."

16

Van was supposed to be on his way to work, but could not stop himself from coming here knowing he might get a glimpse of Bishop after the church service was over.

He was angry with himself. This had not been the first time he waited here, hoping to just see him and maybe have the courage to approach, have a conversation like they used to. Those were some of Van's favorite memories: sitting together in a park, his car, or a hotel room, just talking like father and son.

"Something's on your mind, son," Van remembered Bishop saying one warm night while they were drawn in horse carriage down Decatur Street in the French Quarter of New Orleans. It was one of the many business trips Larry took Van with him on.

Van had been staring off into the dark sky when the question was posed. "Un uh, nothing's on my mind," he lied. He felt Bishop's hand on his shoulder, bidding him to face him. When he did, Bishop gave Van a reassuring smile.

"I know you," he said. "You can tell me or ask me anything. You know that."

Van did know that. He had the kind of relationship with this man he never had with another. He relied on Bishop, trusted him. Van loved him as any son would love a father.

"We're gonna be like…like this always, right? You're always gonna be here for me, right?"

Bishop chuckled. Van felt him smooth his hand up and down Van's back. Bishop always knew how to comfort him. "Why would you ask me that?"

"My father...he left me when I was—"

"I know," Bishop said. "Your mother told me, but I won't leave you, son. I love you, and I'll never leave you."

Van woke from his daydream. He had been parked outside the church, around back, near the parking lot for almost half an hour waiting, when finally he saw him. Van cranked his seat back forward and stared transfixed as Bishop Larry Lakes walked toward his car, a half smile on his face, as though he had not a trouble in the world.

Van's hand was on the door handle. He was about to leave the car, take hurried strides across that lot to talk to Bishop, but for no reason it seemed the bishop slowed, then stopped suddenly. As if sensing someone's eyes on him, he turned to his left, spotting Van's old Honda Civic.

Van thought to duck, hide from the man's view, but thought again. There was no secret between them. Van knew what had him drive his car there; Van knew Bishop was equally aware.

The man continued to stand and stare, holding Van's glare from twenty yards away, as if daring him to make the next move.

Van pulled on the door handle, began to push it open, then stopped. His heart thumped in his chest and he felt out of breath. He had dreamt of the day when he would speak to Bishop again; every word he wanted to speak was memorized in his head. Now they were gone. He pulled the door shut, started the car and pulled off.

As he drove away, he saw that Bishop did not take another step, just continued to watch Van till he was out of sight.

Fifteen minutes later, Van yanked open the door and hurried into the U-Stop gas station convenience store only seven minutes late, but late enough, he knew, to catch all hell from his boss.

The busted 91' Honda Civic stopped on the side of the street again, smoke billowing from under the hood. Van had to grab the empty jug out the hatch, find water, then fill the car's radiator and wait for the piece of junk to cool down before he could start it up again.

"Arjun, Arjun," Van called, hurrying past an old black lady standing at the counter waiting to be served. A young boy, holding six bags of twenty-five cent chips, stood behind her.

"Arjun, I'm here," Van said, stopping in front of the open door of the small back office.

Arjun Gupta, a clean-shaven Indian man in his late twenties sat behind a tiny desk, lazily tapping the keys on a laptop computer.

"Sorry I'm late, Arjun," Van said. "But my car—"

Wearing a black wife beater t-shirt, Arjun glanced up at the clock on the wall. His tone low and even, his Indian accent thick, he said, "You're fucking ten minutes late. Those customers been waiting at the counter for you."

"Then why ain't you take care of 'em?"

"Because it's your fucking job. Now get up there and do it!"

Van turned, and stomped back through the aisles of can goods and plastic packaged foods. He stepped behind the counter, apologized to the elderly woman waiting and rang up her purchases.

For the next two hours Van sat behind the bulletproof glass in his little cage, surrounded by scratch-off lottery tickets, cigarette products and porno magazines, staring out at the gas pumps.

He eyed a group of men standing in a circle outside in the gas station parking lot, looking like they were up to no good. One caught Van's stare and mean-mugged him, shrugged his shoulders like he wanted to pick a fight. Van turned away, feeling like a failure for working such a dead end job.

Years ago, he had tried community college; he was elated when he was accepted. He took Sierra with him to the CVS to buy his school supplies, telling her how he was planning on getting his masters degree after he finished the bachelors. But while sitting in class, he couldn't get his mind to function, to do the stuff it was supposed to do.

"You can do the work," Sierra tried to convince him after he had showed her his third failing test paper in a row. "You just have to know that you can. You have to have confidence in yourself."

But that was what he was lacking most.

Van withdrew from school after only four weeks. He failed then and was a failure now, and he could not attribute that to anyone but the man who abandoned him and left Van feeling worthless. He couldn't even afford to keep enough food in the house for his wife and starving child.

Van stepped out of the cashier's room and walked down the narrow hall again that led to Arjun's office. He stopped in the doorway and stared at the man.

Arjun looked up from his computer. "What do you want?"

"I need a loan till payday. Now before you say no, I'm just saying, I wouldn't be asking if I—"

Arjun stood, stepped out from behind his desk, walked over to Van and said, "Get out of my office. I pay you for the time you work here. You spend it all in one day, that's not my—"

"Arjun!" Van said. "I ain't asking you to *give* me money, I just need a loan. Take it out of my next check."

Arjun stepped in Van's face, as though he would walk through him if Van did not step out the office. Van backed just outside the office door.

"You get paid on payday. Now get back to work," Arjun said, closing the door in Van's face.

Walking toward the cashier's room, Van glanced up at the security cameras in the convenience store. They fed back to a monitor in Arjun's office. Van knew every now and again Arjun would glance up at the monitor, but most times Arjun paid it no mind. Van halted in the middle of the store surrounded by so much food, food that he and his family desperately needed. Food that Arjun would not give Van an advance to pay for. He tried to do things the right way, but Arjun left him with no choice.

17

Marian sat at a wooden park table eating a cup of vanilla ice cream with a plastic spoon as she watched Jabari give Simone a piggyback ride on the grassy area some thirty feet away.

"Feeling better?" Paul asked, sitting across the table wearing a tan linen suit, his hair particularly curly today. Marian noticed he hadn't shaved, and a faint shadow of hair dirtied his sculptured cheeks, chin and jaw.

This whole ice cream thing was Paul's idea; twenty minutes ago Marian was vehemently against it.

"I said where are you taking us?" Marian practically shouted from the back seat of the Town Car.

"Don't worry about it," Paul said, making turns she knew would not lead them back to the mansion, where they were supposed to have been taken after Sunday service. The kids were in the back seat with Marion seeming not to care that the man had kidnapped them; they were enjoying the ride on the sunny day.

Marian leaned up on the back of the front seat. "Paul, if you do not stop this car this very minute, you will be out of a job!" At that point, Marian was fed up and pissed off. It was bad enough that her husband forgot her freaking anniversary last night and ignored almost every word she said, but for the hired help, her personal assistant to do it—absolutely not!

Paul turned another corner and pulled into a small shopping center.

"Ooh, ice cream!" the kids cried. "Mommy, can we have some?"

Paul slowly pulled in a parking spot beside the Bruster's ice cream hut, where a line of parents and children waited to be served. He shut off the car then looked over the seat at Marian. "Let's get the kids some ice cream. You can fire me afterward."

In answer to Paul's question as to whether she felt better, the answer was a definite yes. The sun was shining, her children were laughing and happy, and despite what happened at church today, not to mention the ridiculous number of calories she was taking in, Marian felt better. She smiled. "Yes, I'm feeling a little better."

"I'm glad," Paul said, licking the top of his cone.

"You don't run this. You work for me, remember?" Marian half-joked. "If I tell you to take us home, you take us home."

"Yes, ma'am," Paul smiled.

It was a beautiful smile, showing straight white teeth, Marian thought. "I'm serious," she said. "I won't tolerate insubordination."

"You won't have to tell me again." Paul stood from the bench and held his cone out to her. "I need to get something from the trunk. Can you hold this?"

Marian took the cone, wondering what Paul was up to as she watched him walk to the Town Car, go in the trunk and walk back with a beautiful, colorful bouquet of spring flowers.

He set them on the table just in front of her and took his cone back.

"What…what is this?" Marian asked, already enjoying the scent of the roses, lilies and carnations.

"It was your anniversary the other night, right? So I bought you flowers," Paul said, taking his seat like what he did was no big deal. Like a personal assistant was expected to buy his married employer a lovely bouquet of flowers for her anniversary.

"It's not your place," Marian scolded. She was all of a sudden angry. Not because of Paul's purchase, but because he got her flowers when her husband didn't.

"You don't like them?"

"I didn't say that. They're...they're beautiful, but I can't accept them."

Paul took the flowers back, set them on the bench beside him, out of Marian's sight. "I'll throw them away before we leave then."

"No," Marian said. "Don't you have a girlfriend to give them to?"

Paul took another lick of his cone, seeming no longer interested in it. "Used to. We were together three years. She was beautiful. I asked her to marry me. She said yes," Paul smiled, wistfully. "I saved for a whole year and bought her a ring. You wanna see it?"

Marian nodded.

Paul reached into the collar of his shirt, pulled out the tiny link, silver chain he wore. On the end of it was an engagement ring with a narrow, silver band and a cloudy diamond so small Marian had to squint to see it. He leaned over the table, holding it out to give her a better look.

She could smell just a hint of his cologne as she examined the ring. She breathed in deep. "Nice," Marian said, holding the ring, realizing she would've happily accepted a ring just like it from a man who loved her as much as it seemed Paul loved the girl he was talking about.

"So what happened?" Marian asked, letting go of the ring.

Paul frowned. "Walked in on her with some dude." His eyes were closed as if he was reliving the moment. Marian hoped that wasn't what he was doing.

"I'm so sorry," she said.

He opened his eyes, smiled a little. "It was almost a year ago. I'm over it. She had a little boy and girl, around the same ages as yours. I miss them. Maybe that's why I've taken so much to your kids."

Marian didn't comment, but she was aware of all the time and attention he spent on Jabari and Simone and the joy he seemed to get from them. When she looked up, Paul was staring in her eyes. "You okay?" she asked him.

"I treated her the best I could. I loved her with everything I had, but she couldn't do right by me. I ask myself sometimes what the hell that was about?"

Marian could see how hurt he was, and if she weren't a married, devoted woman, she would've reached across that table, given him a hug and tried her best to console him. "Things will get better."

"Yeah, I know. But right now, I guess I'm just tired of being alone." Paul stood, fished the car keys out of his pocket. "Come on, I need to be getting you and the kids back home."

18

Van turned the knob on his apartment door, praying his wife and baby were asleep.

When he walked in, Sierra was sitting up in bed looking fearful, a shoe in her hand, held over her head to defend herself and her baby against an intruder.

"It's me, it's me," Van said, knowing she wasn't expecting anyone to be coming through their door at this time of the afternoon.

"What...what are you doing home?" Sierra said, sleep in her voice. Van had obviously woken her up.

He glanced toward the crib. Virgil was still napping.

Van sat down on the mattress, set his book bag down at his feet, gave his wife a hug, kissed her face then lay down the small bouquet of flowers he bought at the Kroger food store. They were wilted, but they were discounted 50 percent, so they didn't cut too much into the money he had stolen.

Van wrapped his arms around his wife. Sierra's skin was warm. She held her arms down at her side, as if more concerned about Van being home than his display of affection.

"What are those for?" she asked.

"To show you that I love you. Don't worry, they weren't that much."

Sierra picked up the flowers, sniffed them. She tried to deny it, but Van saw that she liked them. That pleased him.

She looked sadly at him. "Thank you, but why the hell are you here?"

"Sierra, look—"

"No, no. Please tell me you still have a job, Van."

"Sierra, look—" Van said, reaching for his wife's hand.

She pushed him away, stood from the bed wearing boxers and a purple bra. "What happened? Just tell me! I'm tired of all these secrets with you," she said, hysteria in her voice.

"Fine." Van grabbed his book bag, unzipped it and dumped food onto the bed.

"What is this? Where did it come from?" Sierra set down the flowers and pushed through the food.

"Does it matter?"

At work, standing in the middle of the store, having decided that having food now was worth more to him than the shitty treatment and shitty pay he'd receive from Arjun later, Van grabbed his book bag from the corner of the cashier's room and hurried down the aisles of the store, filling the bag with canned goods, bottles of baby food, bags of chips, and packages of cookies. He ran to the freezers and dumped several cans of soda into the bag till it was full.

He zipped it up, shouldered it, then hurried back into the cashier's room, opened the register and snatched all the cash out—what Van believed amounted to almost $60.

"We didn't have any food so I got us some. And here…" Van said, digging out of his pocket what was left of the crumpled, stolen money. "I got us this, too."

"I don't want that! I wanna know where this food came from. I wanna know why you ain't at work. Do you still have a job, Van?"

Van paced away from the bed. "I'm working there everyday, ain't making no real money. We don't have no food. My family is starving. I had to do something."

"Just answer me, please!"

"I stole the food and the money!" Van turned shouting, his hands, for some reason tightened into fists at his sides.

A tear raced down Sierra's cheek. She stood beside the bed, trembling. "No. We aren't making it now. We behind on the rent. There's no food in this house. The milk I fed Virgil before he went down was more than half water. You gotta go back to work."

"I can't. Arjun is gonna find out I stole from him and…I can't get my job back."

"So what are we supposed to do? We have a baby. A baby you said it was okay to have. Do you remember that?" Sierra said, stepping over to Van, stopping just in front of him. "Do you remember telling me that you would take care of us if we got pregnant?"

How could he forget, over a year ago lying in bed with Sierra?

The thoughts, memories and regrets were beating him up pretty badly that day. Everything he tried to shut them up didn't work. She was telling him about her girlfriend who was seven months pregnant. Sierra rubbed her flat, bare belly and smiled. "I wonder what it would feel like to have one inside me?"

Van needed more to do, more responsibility, something to keep his mind from wandering back to those horrible events. What Sierra was talking about—a responsibility like that—he could handle. He could be a father, a good one, and through his efforts, maybe he could erase the pain that was done to him. But it was more than that. This hadn't been the first time Sierra had hinted at wanting to get pregnant. It was something he knew she truly wanted, and all he wanted to do was make her happy.

He turned to her. "I can give you one."

"What?"

"A baby."

"But we barely making it. We ain't got the money to take care of—"

Van pulled Sierra close, kissed her lips. "I'd be a good father. I wouldn't let our baby go hungry. I'd be the best father," he said, needing her to know that. "And I love you. It'll be good for us. Let me give you a baby. I promise I'll take care of us. We'll be fine."

It took a moment, but a smile appeared on Sierra's face. She reached for Van, pulled him on top, kissed his lips and opened her legs.

"Van," he heard Sierra call, snatching him from his thoughts. "This life is shit!" she said, wiping tears that were now dripping from her face. "But you have to make it better because you told me you would."

She was putting this all on him, but it wasn't just his fault.

"Van, we are going to be put out on the street if you don't have a job!"

Didn't she realize none of this was his fault?

"Goddammit, Van! Are you fucking listening? You have to do something!"

He could take no more and Van was up on top of the mattress, his feet sinking into the cushion as he stormed across it. He grabbed Sierra, slammed her against the wall, his hand around her throat, strangling her. He heard her gagging. Virgil was screaming now; the baby must've woken. Tears crawled down Van's face. "I can't do nothing! I can't! Do you know what I'm going through? Every fucking day, do you know what's in my head?" he yelled.

"No," Sierra gasped, her face reddish purple, her hands around his wrists, clawing at them to be released. "Tell me!"

"No. No!" He whipped his head back and forth, crying. He punched the wall just beside his wife's head, leaving a speck of blood on the crumbled plaster. He released her, and heard her choking for air as he ran out of the apartment door.

19

Late that night, Larry stood in one of the small basement rooms of the church, his hands clasped behind his back, wearing slacks and a jacket he had hurriedly thrown over a sweatshirt. A bare bulb hung from the ceiling casting bright light on the cement walls, floor and the thief cuffed to the chair.

The sight of the boy made Larry think back to one of the days when he starved as a child.

Larry was thirteen, and he stood in the kitchen of the small rental unit after he'd finished making the sandwich of bologna and bread—items he had stuffed under his shirt and stolen from the small corner store two blocks away.

Larry hadn't heard Lincoln walk in, but he heard his deep, angry voice behind him when his father asked, "Where did you get that food?"

Larry's mouth was open, the sandwich held in both his hands, just inches from his face. He pulled it away and spun around to see his father standing angrily in the doorway.

"Don't lie to me, boy," Lincoln said, walking up to Larry, stopping a few feet in front of him.

Larry's eyes rested on Lincoln's right hand, knowing what was coming if he lied and his father found out. "I was hungry and I stole—"

The huge, open hand across Larry's face came before he could finish admitting his guilt. The sandwich flew to the floor, Larry spiraling down after it. He sat there, crying as his father wrapped up the stolen goods. He dragged Larry by the hand back to the store where Lincoln apologized to the manager.

"He'll take whatever punishment you decide," Lincoln said, holding Larry by his collar like a disobedient dog. "The boy has to learn right from wrong."

In the basement of Holy Sweet Spirit Church, Tyrell Suggs stood beside Larry. He had called him just as he was lying down for bed.

"What is it?" Larry said, glancing at the bedside clock. It read 11:02 p.m.

Marian had already dozed off beside him. He definitely didn't want to wake her.

Rolling over an hour before, turning her back on Larry to go to sleep, Marian had let him know just how disappointed she was in him asking for additional help from the congregation. Again, he told her how much in need the family and the church were.

"Sad thing is," Marian said. "It's not even that you asked them for the money. They gladly gave, so you got what you wanted, I guess. It's just that you don't even listen to a word I say anymore. Sometimes I wonder what use I am to you."

Marian didn't wait for an answer, just rolled over and clicked off her lamp.

An hour later, Larry was woken up by the call from Tyrell Suggs.

Now Larry stood looking at the thief, thinking that the boy must've suffered some seriously hard times in the few years since he had last seen him.

The heavyset security guard, a man named Benny, had briefed Larry five minutes ago, just outside the door.

"Heard some noise out around back," Officer Benny Payton said. "When I went out there, I saw the guy cutting copper wire away from the air conditioning unit."

The copper the young man did manage to cut away lay alongside the left wall of the room.

"Urail," Larry said, speaking for the first time since entering. "Why were you trying to steal from the church?"

Urail's eyes had never left Larry since he stepped in. He wore an old winter coat, rain boots and dirty clothes underneath. He was no longer the clean, handsome boy Larry had recruited for his boy's youth ministry. He looked like a stranger.

"Answer the question, Urail. We could've called the police, but I was told you wanted to speak to me, so I came over here to—"

"You wrong, Bishop," Urail finally said. "For making us—"

"I don't know what you're talking about!" Larry said, taking two forceful steps toward Urail.

"You wrong!" Urail said again.

"What's he talking about, Bishop?" Officer Payton asked.

"Obviously, there's something wrong with him mentally," Larry said.

"You wrong for what you did to us, and you gotta—"

"Urail!" Larry said, quieting the young man. Larry reached into his back pocket, pulled out his wallet. "You're experiencing hard times. We can see that. But once being a member of this church, you could've just called and asked for assistance. You didn't have to go trying to steal from us just to make a few dollars," Larry said, fishing two crisp twenty-dollar bills from his billfold. He held them out before Urail's eyes, folded them then slid them into the breast pocket of the boy's dirty, plaid shirt. "Now get him up."

Tyrell Suggs and Officer Payton grabbed either of Urail's arms and stood him from the chair.

"Boy needs a bath something serious," Tyrell Suggs said.

Larry faced Urail, stared deep into his eyes. They stared back empty, unblinking. It appeared to Larry as though no one was there.

"Urail, are you okay?"

Urail continued to stare into Larry's eyes without speaking a word. Finally Larry caught a glimpse of the boy he used to know—the boy he used to consider a son.

"When was the last time you had something to eat? Where do you sleep at night?" Larry asked.

"Whopper Jr. yesterday, I think," Urail said.

Larry shook his head, deeply saddened. "And where are you sleeping?"

Urail looked around the room as if considering one of the corners as a possible place to bed down. "Wherever," he said.

"Benny," Larry said, grabbing the big officer by the arm and leading him over to the other side of the room. Tyrell Suggs followed. Larry's voice lowered, he instructed the man to, "Give the boy some towels. Let him clean up in the bathroom, and make up the bed in the rectory so he can sleep there tonight."

"Bishop," Tyrell Suggs said. "He tried to steal from you, and you gonna let him wash his ass and stay up in here?"

"He was a member of this church. 'Come to me, all you who are weary and burdened, and I will give you rest. Lord said it, so that's what we gonna do. Payton," Larry said, turning to the big man. "You hear what I said?"

"Yes sir," Officer Payton said.

"I think you making a big mistake, Bishop," Tyrell Suggs said.

"I don't know, but I'm not just going to have him wandering the streets. And one more thing," Larry said, catching Officer Payton before he stepped away. "Don't listen to a word the boy says. He has a wild imagination and some pretty serious mental problems. He's liable to say anything."

20

"Sit down, Officer Gentry," the commander of the Fulton County Jail told Robby on Monday morning.

Robby took his seat knowing the kind of trouble he was in. Officer Oaks and Gerald sat in the small conference room as well, both men glaring angrily at Rasheed Jenkins.

Jenkins sat on the other side of the table, a patch covering his left eye and stitches sewn into his lip. His face was bruised and swollen; white gauze was wrapped several times over the top of his head, under his chin and over the top of his head again. He appeared as though he had been beaten with baseball bats, which Robby knew he pretty much was. Jenkins's wrists were cuffed behind his back, and he wore a cast that stretched from the toes of his right foot all the way up his leg to just below his hip.

"What's the problem, Commander?" Robby said, without acknowledging his co-workers or the shackled inmate.

Commander Riley was tall, lean and wore a crew cut. He shook his head and leaned back in his chair. "I'm ready to have the three of you fired for beating and threatening to rape this inmate."

Robby glanced at Gerald and Oaks. Their faces were hardened, probably feeling as though their jobs wouldn't have been in jeopardy if not for Robby dragging them into the mess.

"We didn't do anything, Commander," Robby said. "That piece of shit is nothing but a lying, worthless, rapist who—"

"Stop it, Gentry," Riley said. "The jail has cameras we don't even tell the officers about just for this kind of thing. It was steamy in there, but I saw the whole thing."

Robby turned his eyes downward.

"What about you, Gerald? Oaks?" Riley questioned. "Why the fuck would you do something like this?"

"Like Gentry said, he raped another inmate and—" Gerald began.

"And what?" Riley said. "You've been working here long enough to know that happens every fucking day, and there is a protocol for that which doesn't include beating the offender within an inch of his life." Riley stood from the table, dragged a hand down his face and sighed loudly. "If the higher-ups get a hold of this the three of you are definitely gone. But I don't want to do that."

"Then don't," Robby said.

"And do what?" Riley said. "Because something's definitely gonna be done."

"Then whatever it is, just do it to me," Robby said. "I brought this thing to Gerald and Oaks. They wouldn't have even known if I hadn't told them, so…"

Riley looked over to the other officers. "That true?"

"We were there just like Gentry was so we deserve—"

"Just answer the fucking question, Oaks," Riley said.

"Gentry asked for our help so we helped him," Oaks admitted. "Assholes like Jenkins need to know just because he likes a dick up the ass, doesn't mean everyone else does."

Commander Riley walked over, stood beside Rasheed Jenkins, glaring down at him like he would've taken a shot at him if he wasn't responsible for setting the example around there. He grimaced when he said, "Although you will still face disciplinary action for the assault of another inmate, I apologize for what my men did to you. It's expected that *you* should behave like a fucking animal—not my men." Riley turned to his officers. "Oaks, Gerald, take this human waste back to his cell. Gentry and I need to have a talk."

Officer Gerald grabbed inmate Jenkins by the arm, yanked him out of the chair and pushed him in the direction of the door.

"Thanks man," Officer Oaks said, slapping Robby on the back before stepping out of the room and closing him in with Riley.

Commanding Officer Riley took his seat at the table opposite Robby. He shook his head. "What the fuck is wrong with you, Gentry? This is not the first time you've done something as boneheaded as this. You need more counseling? Is something wrong with you? You need a goddamn psychiatric evaluation?"

The answer to all those questions was yes, Robby thought. "Hell no, sir," Robby said. "I just don't like…why would a man—"

"Who fucking knows? It's jail, Gentry. Been happening since there've been jails, and probably before. You beating up every asshole that does it isn't going to help." Riley stood and paced around the table. "You're a good C.O. most of the time, so I'm not going to shit can you. But I'm suspending you. For a month without pay."

"What?" Robby said, standing from his chair. "But I need—"

"Sit down! And you should've thought about the money you'd lose before you tried playing Batman in my jail." Riley took the seat beside Robby, stared him in the eyes. "Take the time, get whatever help you need. Come back here fixed. Because you're sure as hell broken." Riley stood, walked to the door, opened it. "And when you return, do anything thing like this again, not only will I fire your ass, I'll bring you up on charges and see that your ass lands in a cell."

His head down, Robby exited the door of the jail building carrying a box with the belongings from his locker he would not be able to do a month without.

He turned and pushed his way out the doors of the prison, thankful for the sunlight. He walked the distance to the prison gate that surrounded the compound then stopped suddenly surprised to see the person waiting just outside of that gate. It had been more than three years since he had laid eyes on him.

Back and forth, Urail shifted his weight from one leg to the other as if having to pee very badly. He wore a fur-lined winter coat despite the warm weather, and black rubber boots, his filthy jeans stuffed into the tops. He lowered the hood from his long, uncombed hair, and smiled, showing Robby yellowing teeth.

"Robby," Urail said. "We need to talk about Bishop."

21

Marian sat in the Town Car staring up at the second floor
balcony and a row of apartment doors. In particular, she eyed apartment
201. It was the door Paul unlocked and stepped into ten minutes ago.
They had just dropped Jabari and Simone off at school when he realized
he had forgotten his wallet at home.

"You mind if I swing by and grab it?" Paul asked, apology in his
voice.

"Do we have a choice? You need your license, right?" Marian
said, fed up, her frustration not with Paul, but with her husband.

This morning, Larry was late to breakfast. Although Marian's
mother didn't seem to miss him, the kids were asking where their father
was. When Larry finally made an appearance, he was hurrying. He
kissed the kids, took two huge gulps of Jabari's orange juice, stole one of
Simone's sausage links and was heading toward the front door. Marian
was right behind him, caught him with his hand on the doorknob.

"What are you doing?" she asked. "You can't even spend five
minutes with the kids before dashing out like the house was on fire?"

"Marian, I'm sorry," Larry said, chewing the last of the sausage.
"I have a very important meeting today regarding the new church."

"Like the important meeting you had last night," Marian said.
"When you climbed out of bed at nearly midnight."

"That was church business I had—"

"Isn't it always Larry," Marian said. "You're still going to make
it to the counseling session I made for us today, right?"

"Yeah, Marian. I told you I would, so I will," Larry said.

Marian refocused her attention on apartment door 201, her hand on the car's door handle. She scanned the neighborhood. The car was parked in the southeast side of Atlanta—the rough end. Trash and ragged cars littered the curbs. A liquor and convenience store sat just across the street; a group of old men huddled around the door laughing.

Despite all that, Marian pushed open the door of the Lincoln, climbed the metal stairs and walked across the balcony, stopping in front of door 201. She raised a fist to knock, stopped and tried the doorknob instead. It turned, and she found herself looking into the living room of a small, neatly kept apartment. She walked in, softly pushing the door closed. She thought to call out for Paul, but her curiosity kept her quiet. Secondhand furniture, a small TV, and mismatched bookcases lined with scores of paperbacks filled the small space. Marian took a step further in, when Paul stepped out of his door.

"What are you doing in here?" he said, shocked.

"I...I don't know," Marian said, sincerely. If she had been forced to answer, she imagined she would've told him she just wanted to see the environment he lived in. "You said you just had to get your wallet. You were taking a long time, so..."

"So I got it," Paul said, holding the billfold so she could see it. "Let's go."

"How long have you lived here?" Marian said, deciding she wasn't ready to leave that moment. She walked toward a window and looked out onto a parking lot. She turned back to face Paul. "It's neat. Do you like it here?"

"Why are you asking me these questions?" Paul said, appearing unsettled.

"My husband hired you. I know nothing about you," Marian said, walking into the open, galley kitchen. "And considering you're in my house everyday, and I'm trusting you to drive my children around, don't you think I should know who you are?" She pulled open his fridge and looked inside.

Paul was quickly behind her, closing the door in her face.

Marian turned, stood in front of Paul. "So, you going to answer the questions?"

"No, I'm not. You don't need to know anymore about me. The information your husband needed from me in order to get hired, I gave him. If that's not enough, maybe you should let me go."

To Marian, Paul spoke rougher to her than he normally did. "You're upset with me. I do something wrong?"

Frustrated, Paul said, "You...you broke into my place."

"I didn't break in."

"I didn't let you in, so you broke in," Paul said, stepping closer to Marian. "You're in my place, and you know how..." Paul trailed off, staring deep into Marian's eyes then down at her lips. He was breathing heavily, panting almost, but managed to turn away.

"I know how what?" Marian asked, even though she had some idea of what Paul was going to say. She saw that he wanted to reach out, take her in his arms and kiss her, but he fought that urge because she had warned him he would be fired if he ever made another advance on her.

"Nothing," Paul said, looking at her again, almost angrily. "If you're done looking around my place, I think we should go."

22

"Van, you don't look good, baby," Van's mother, Samantha said. He sat across from her in the living room of her apartment. She was only forty, but she looked ten years older—her eyes tired. Gray hair already sprouted long from the roots of her head. She was still attractive, always had been, and Van knew that was the reason for her aging so fast—dealing with the drama that came with all the men that were attracted to her.

Van didn't know his father, never met him. Instead, he was introduced to all his mother's "friends," the men he was told to call Uncle—the men who stayed around for a couple of months, only to be replaced by other men.

Samantha was deeply religious, had herself and her boy in church every Sunday, even though Saturday nights, she was either gone or in the bedroom with the door closed, the TV volume up to mask the screams and moans of sexual passion.

"I'm fine, Mama," Van said, noticing his mother didn't look too good either, which made him feel worse about the reason he was there.

"How is Sierra? She still in school?"

"Yeah, Mama. She's good. Still working nights and school in the morning."

Samantha nodded. "Yes, that girl is a little go-getter. You're lucky to have her. You know that?"

"I know, Mama."

"I was gonna go to school like her, but I didn't."

"I know, Mama."

"And how is my beautiful, big-headed grandson?" Samantha asked, smiling, full of pride. "He talkin yet?"

"Not yet, but he's trying," Van said, feeling a stab of pain, remembering just the other night standing over his son, a gun pointed to his face.

"I remember when you were little like that."

"Me too," Van said sadly, feeling that the only thing that brought his mother joy now were memories.

"I remember the first time I dressed you up for kindergarten pictures, you were in a little tie and jacket. Oh, how you hated those clothes. Even when you were older, the first time we went to the new church, you still hated dressing up. You remember?"

How could he forget? His mind took him back there, when he was fifteen years old, after that service. He and his mother stood in the foyer, just outside the sanctuary, when a handsome man approached them. It was the bishop of the church. He stood in front of them, smiling a moment without saying a word. Confidence radiated from him. He extended his hand and Samantha quickly, gratefully took it. For a moment Van thought she would kneel and kiss his knuckles. They introduced themselves.

"And this must be your son," the bishop said, eyeing Van approvingly.

"Yes," Samantha said, resting a hand on Van's shoulder. "This is Van."

The bishop held out a hand. Van paused, for some reason remembering the warning he was taught in first grade—"Never speak to strangers." This man felt like a stranger. But Van shook, then pulled back his hand the moment the bishop released it.

Bishop Lakes smiled. "Well, Ms. Myers, I think your son would be perfect for our boy's ministry. Please consider that for him. I'm sure he would enjoy it."

"Yes, I will do that, Bishop. Thank you," Samantha said, lustfully watching the man walk away till he disappeared around a corner.

Van sat on the edge of Samantha's sofa in silence. His eyes refocused on his mother. She was sitting, staring quietly at him, concern on her face.

He smiled uncomfortably. "Hey. You okay?"

"Yeah, but you aren't. You were doing it again. Staring off into space—gone. I called you several times, but you didn't say anything."

"No, Mama, you didn't."

"I did. What's wrong? I knew there was something wrong the minute you stepped in here."

Rather than tell her what had been wrong for so long, Van told her what was wrong now. "I lost my job. I need to borrow some money."

Samantha looked at her son like she knew there was more to it than what she was being told. She stood up, went to the drawer of the desk in the dining room and came back with a narrow roll of dollars, a green rubber band around it. She put it in her son's hand. "It's not quite two hundred dollars. It's all I have."

23

Richard Bonner, the mayor of Union City, was a large, light brown man with reddish-brown hair and freckles spotting his chubby face. He sat in front of Larry in the low-lit downtown hotel restaurant enjoying the steak filet lunch Larry invited him to weeks ago. Over his large suit hung a cloth napkin he had stuffed into the collar of his shirt. To Larry he looked like a fifty-five-year-old, newborn baby at feeding time. Mayor Bonner set his knife and fork down on his empty plate, licked his fingers, then pulled the napkin from his collar and wiped his hands and face.

"That was good," he said, waving over the waitress who stood in the back of the restaurant. She appeared at the table.

"You can take this. I'm done with it."

The waitress, a young woman wearing a white shirt, bowtie and a dark vest, gathered up the dishes and wiped the spilled crumbs and gravy from the table.

"And bring me another Jim Beam and ice when you come back," Mayor Bonner said, picking up the glass of Jim Beam he already had and sipped from it. "Now you were saying, Bishop."

"Mayor, I was saying that construction on my new church has been stalled for over a month and—"

"I told you, zoning—"

"Enough with that zoning stuff. Just tell me what I need to do to get my church finished."

Mayor Bonner sighed heavily, tilted his glass up and sucked on a few of the ice cubes.

"I met with the Union City church leaders," Larry said.

"And they don't like you," Mayor Bonner finished for him.

"Tell me something I don't already know."

"And they don't want you there."

"I know that, but—"

"There is no but, Larry," Mayor Bonner said. "Those are my people and the thousands of people that attend their churches are my people, too. I have to take care of them. They've been here for years and years, so I can't just let some new guy come in and take what they've got."

"Take what they've got? I'm just trying to minister to the people."

Mayor Bonner let out a loud belly laugh. The waitress came with his drink, set it down in front of him. He lifted it with a fat hand and took two gulps. "That's all you're trying to do, huh? You're a cancer. You come in and infect everything around you. Their words, not mine," Mayor Bonner said.

"It's them just trying to keep me out. None of that is true."

"There are grumblings about some girl who goes to your church filing molestation charges against you."

Surprise covered Larry's face. How did Mayor Bonner find out about that?

"News gets around, Larry," Mayor Bonner said, reading the question on Larry's face. "Even the sensitive kind, if you know the right people."

"So that's the way you're going to do it? The hundreds of thousands of dollars I have invested in this, I'm going to lose? There is nothing, absolutely nothing I can do to make things work?" Larry asked, knowing there had to have been something. He was familiar with Bonner's reputation. He loved money, would cut under-the-table deals whenever possible to finance his expensive taste for fine clothes, nice cars, beautiful women and his huge house.

"Like I said Larry, the church leaders in my town don't like you very much. It would be ill-advised for me to go against them. They are taxpayers. The city receives a lot of money from those churches."

"My church will be twice as big as any of those. Your city will make a lot of money from it. Maybe even a little extra left over for you. That is..." Larry said, leaning in toward the mayor, "...if it can be guaranteed that the building of my church will not be interrupted again."

"Excuse me gentleman, I just wanted to check on you two, make sure that everything is wonderful," Shreeva said, standing beside the table. She wore a close- fitting, simple white gown with a neckline that plunged almost to the bottom of her sternum. Her breasts looked so round, so full and so perfect in that dress that Mayor Bonner could not take his eyes from them.

"I'm fine, Shreeva," Larry said. Shreeva worked as the hostess at the hotel restaurant, got them to open it early for this meeting. It was all her idea. When Larry told Shreeva that he believed Bonner was the man halting the completion of his church, Shreeva offered to help him with the problem.

"I heard he's a woman chaser," Shreeva said, over drinks in her condo, weeks ago. "Maybe he would be interested in chasing me."

"I don't want you to have to do that," Larry said. "I'll find a way to work—"

"I know the way," Shreeva said, bouncing in her seat, making her breasts jump under her shirt. "Let's just get this done, get the church built so I can assume my rightful place by your side."

"Are you sure about this?" Larry said.

"I'm sure I want us to be together, Daddy. You said the only way that's going to happen is if you finish the church," Shreeva said, staring at Larry, seriousness on her face. "So, yeah baby, I'm serious."

Shreeva decided to wear the little dress in the attempt to entice the mayor, just in case money alone would not sway him to do Larry's bidding.

"And how about you, Mayor?" Shreeva said, walking behind the big man, resting her hands on his shoulders and gently massaging him.

The man giggled like a fool. "Oh, oh…good, very good."

Shreeva leaned over, pressing her bare cleavage against his left ear. "Well if there is anything, and I do mean anything I can do to make it better, you just let me know."

"Yes…yeah, okay," Mayor Bonner said. He watched with unblinking eyes as Shreeva switched her way across the restaurant and into the double doors of the kitchen.

Larry stared at Mayor Bonner as he watched the doors swing back and forth.

"So Mayor," Larry finally said, snapping the man out of his trance. "I really should be going. We can discuss the particulars later. But do we have a deal?"

"You know that woman?" Mayor Bonner said, his eyes still on the double doors.

"Yes, I know her very well."

"Are you…you know?" Bonner said, looking up at Larry. He slowly extended a fist to simulate thrusting hips.

"No," Larry lied.

"Do you think she'd…give me some time?"

"You're the mayor of Union City, Georgia," Larry said. "A very powerful man. She might if I convinced her."

Mayor Bonner glanced back at the double doors, swallowed the last of his drink then said, "Give me what you promised before and the girl, and you'll get no more interference building your church."

24

The money his mother had given him the other day was all but spent on bills and food.

Van sat on his apartment floor. He watched his son roll around happily playing with a red ball Van had bought him from the dollar store a day ago.

Yesterday, Van apologized to Sierra, told her he was wrong for putting his hands on her like that. "I'm sorry baby, but it'll never happen again. I promise."

She was dressing for work, pushing a brush through her hair. "I know it won't, or I'll take Virgil and leave your ass and never come back." She set the brush down, walked over and stood in front of Van in her security guard uniform. "I understand that you were mad. I know you hate your job. I hate mine, too. But you have to get it back. We need that money. Can you try to get your job back, Van? For your wife and child."

He couldn't say no to at least trying. "If you can try to find a way to forgive me for being so mean to you."

Sierra wrapped her arms around her husband's waist. "Already forgiven." She raised up on her toes and kissed his lips. "Just get the job back."

This morning Van went to the local library, jumped online and searched the want ads for gigs because there was no way in hell his old boss would give him his job back after Van more or less robbed the man. He was surprised Arjun hadn't sent the police for him. Van assumed, instead, Arjun would just keep his last check.

Online, Van found nothing he qualified for so on the way back home, he stopped at the nearest grocery store, Target and Wal-Mart to apply on the computers they had pushed up in corners of the stores. He didn't know why, but he believed he had no hope of getting any of the jobs he had applied for. Before calling it quits, he stopped at two gas stations to ask about work and was rudely told that they weren't hiring.

Now he sat watching his son, playing with not a care in the world, having no idea of how rough life will be for him with such a loser as a father.

Van stared into the space in front of him, let his mind wander back to when there was someone who would help him when times were hard.

He had only been part of Bishop Lake's boy's ministry for a few weeks, but the Bishop took a serious liking to him. He had already taken Van out twice to lunch and once to dinner, in restaurants nicer than Van ever thought existed. They had white table cloths and waiters that pulled your seat out before you sat down.

One particular night, Van rode beside Bishop Lakes in the back seat of his Bentley, on his way to being dropped off at home.

"Next time, I'm going take you to one of my favorite spots downtown. You ever had seafood?"

Van was melancholy, and Bishop Lakes picked up on his mood change right away, asking him what was wrong.

"The people in those places be dressing nice, and I..." Van looked at the tattered jeans he wore, the shirt that was too small and the shoes that were worn in so badly the should've been thrown away long ago.

Bishop Lakes smiled, placed a hand on Van's shoulder. "Don't worry, son. I think I'll be able to do something about that."

The next day after school, Van was picked up in the Bentley again, and Bishop Lakes took Van to Lenox Mall, located in the rich part of town.

Van had never been there. He looked up at the colorful stores, the bright lights and all the nice merchandise—shirts, slacks, jackets—that was sold behind their windows.

"Why did we come here?" Van asked.

"Because you're going shopping, son," Bishop Lakes said.

Van felt the man's reassuring arm around his shoulder again.

"Let's go into whatever stores you want," Bishop Lakes said, "And buy whatever you like. Doesn't matter how much."

Van was startled out of his thoughts by a knock. He stood, scooped Virgil up and carried him in the bend of his arm to the door. When he opened it, a clean-shaven, tall, brown man, wearing a gray suit stood before Van.

"Van Meyers?"

"Yeah, that's me."

The man reached into his suit jacket, pulled out an envelope and handed it to Van.

"What's this?"

"A job is in there, along with the date, time, an address, and how to get there." The man glanced at the baby in Van's arm. "You need a job, right?"

"Who are you?" Van said, wondering if he should've opened the door, if he was in any kind of danger.

"It's at a warehouse distribution center. Wear jeans, work boots and bring work gloves. You got boots and gloves?"

"Yeah," Van said.

"Good." The man looked Van from head to toe with slight disapproval. "Don't be late, Van. Jobs don't come knocking at your door very often," the man said, then turned and walked away.

25

Marian sat in the office of Dr. Belinda Thomas, staring up at the clock on the wall. It read 3:22 p.m.

Dr. Thomas was a regal looking woman, who appeared to be in her mid fifties. She sat in the leather chair of an office decorated in soft earth tones. The blinds let just the right amount of late afternoon sun in. The environment was very soothing, but it did little to calm Marian.

"I'm sorry, Dr. Thomas, just let me try calling my husband one more time." Marian grabbed her phone from her purse, dialed Larry once more and waited angrily for him to answer. His voicemail picked up after the fourth ring as it had done the previous three times she tried to reach him since arriving for their appointment.

"Larry, this morning you said you would be here and you're not." Marian saw that the doctor was staring her in the face. "Just...call me when you get this." Marian turned to Dr. Thomas, disconnecting the call. "I'm so sorry for all of this."

"No problem," Dr. Thomas said with a reassuring smile. "It happens all the time. We still have..." she glanced down at her wrist watch. "A little more than half an hour. You and I can always talk."

Marian exhaled, tried to relax a bit in the leather chair and said, "Why not? I'm paying for the hour, right?"

"Sure," Dr. Thomas smiled, still pressing the pen to the yellow pad of paper she had been holding since the beginning of their session. "So we might as well take it from the top. What brings you in today?"

It was a huge question. Marian thought about starting with her husband's two-hour disappearance last night, or maybe the recent absence of sex in their marriage, or the fact that her husband seemed to be spending more time and attention on the church than his family.

"Well..." Marian started, but she was unable to deny the empty chair beside her and all it represented. Larry obviously wasn't there because he no longer gave a damn, so why should she? "I'm sorry, Dr. Thomas," Marian said, grabbing her purse and standing. "This was supposed to be for my husband and myself. It just doesn't make sense if he's not here."

26

Larry sat in the back seat of the Bentley, half a block away from the high school but close enough to see some of the students standing outside on the campus, laughing and talking. Today had been a long day full of plotting and bargaining.

He had just gotten off the phone with Shreeva.

"The mayor called," she had told Larry.

"And?"

"He asked to come over tonight."

"You're going to see him?" Larry asked, feeling a pinch of jealousy.

"Yeah. I'll turn him out. But his fat ass better not catch a heart attack in my bed."

"I know you're trying to help me, but...you don't have to do this if you don't want to."

"I do." Shreeva said then was silent for a moment. "You are still going to marry me, and I am still going to be the first lady of your new church, right?"

"Yeah," Larry said. "If we get this done, then yeah, all that will happen."

"Do you love me, Daddy? Because I love you," she said, sounding reassured by his promise.

"I do," Larry hesitated.

"Good, cause I'm gonna be thinking of you the whole time I'm fucking this whale. Love you."

Larry hung up the phone, settled back in the leather seat of the Bentley, checked his watch then glanced out his window toward the high school. He felt horrible about what Shreeva was doing for him and the reason behind it. She had very specific expectations, and he wasn't sure he could or wanted to meet them. All he knew was that he had already spent hundreds of thousands on that church and it had to be finished. He would deal with what to do with Shreeva, and how it would affect Marian later.

Larry took a number of deep breaths in and exhaled, trying to calm himself. He was anxious and worried about that whale, Mayor Bonner, as Shreeva referred to him. Something the man said at lunch had Larry spooked. Exactly who had told him of the lies that fool girl, Tatiana, was telling about being molested?

After the meeting with Bonner, Larry promptly phoned Tatiana's attorney. He got her voicemail and left her a scathing message, demanding that she call him back unless she wanted to be sued for defamation of character.

Larry had been constantly checking his phone ever since, looking for missed calls.

He couldn't help but glance at the phone again.

"Lawyer chick ain't call you back yet?" Tyrell Suggs asked, looking over at Larry from the driver's seat.

"No. But she better."

That moment, Larry's phone rang. He glanced down at the number. "This is her," Larry said, before answering. "Attorney Michaels," Larry said, attempting to suppress the anger building in him. "You putting information about these allegations out? You talking to people about this?" Larry held the phone pressed tightly to his face as

111

Attorney Michaels denied leaking any information. "Then how am I hearing about it from people other than you?" He didn't give her time to respond. "I promise, if you're trying to start some smear campaign—" Larry paused, listened, seething. "To the media? You will not! Or else what?" Attorney Michaels suggested Larry pay the settlement that was offered or face being sued and taken to court. "To court?" Larry yelled. "Try it and see who ends up the sorry one!"

Larry pulled the phone from his ear and stabbed the END button with his thumb.

His nostrils flaring, he glanced out the window again. "The woman thinks she's going to railroad me."

"She talking bout trying to take you to court?" Tyrell Suggs asked.

"First going to the media," Larry said, frowning. "Then talking about suing me. It's all talk. That poor, broke child and her family are just trying to get some money. They don't wanna take me on, especially when what she's saying are all lies. Ain't nobody lay a hand on that girl."

Larry remembered what his father used to say during some of their toughest times. "Long as you got the will and the want, you can get through anything."

Lincoln had said that after the loud banging came at the front door of a house they had only lived in for ninety days. Larry was twelve. By that age, he and his father had been thrown out of so many places that an unexpected knock would send Larry into a complete panic. The knocking continued as Larry stood in the middle of the living room, frozen with fear as Lincoln stepped out on the porch. Larry heard men identify themselves as sheriffs. They told Lincoln they had an hour to gather up their things; the rest would be set out on the curb. After the exchange, Lincoln closed the door, walked calmly over to Larry, smiling as though he had just had a conversation with a child selling Girl Scout cookies, not the law telling them they'd be on the street once again.

"Daddy, where we gonna go?" Larry asked before his father opened his mouth.

Lincoln smiled, confidently. "All the places out there? There's always somewhere to go, and long as we got the will and want, we can get through anything."

Larry was startled out of his thoughts by a knock on his window. Through the tinted glass he saw Omar, the young man from his boy's ministry, standing outside, wearing a white collared shirt and blue khakis—his school uniform.

Without instructing him, Tyrell Suggs raised the privacy window, separating him from all sights and sounds that would occur in the back seat of the car.

Larry opened the door and with a smile, invited the boy in.

Omar slid into the spacious back seat cabin of the car. He wore a new pair of black Nike Air Jordan Retro basketball shoes and black Dr. Dre Beats high definition headphones around his neck. Each item cost about $300. They were gifts for the boy's birthday—requests he made of Larry when he phoned him on the number Larry told him never to hesitate calling.

Omar's mother worked late hours at a bar, Larry believed. She got little of nothing in pay, but her son had very expensive taste, and had no problem asking for what he wanted. Larry had no issue giving it to him. Omar was a good kid, and Larry loved nothing more than to see the boy's face light up when he received what he had asked for.

"Well, don't you look very handsome today," Larry said, savoring the boy's good looks, then opening his arms. "Now give me a hug."

27

Marian sat under dimmed lights at one end of the dining room table, staring at her husband, who sat at the other end. She held an empty wine glass in her hand. She set it down, grabbed the bottle of Shiraz and poured herself her fourth serving.

Dinner had ended not five minutes ago. Estelle had cleared most of the dishes and had ushered the children upstairs to wash up for bed.

Now Marian sat at the table, not taking her eyes off Larry. He looked uncomfortable.

"Baby, you okay?" Larry said.

"How was your day?"

He fidgeted with the rings on his fingers. "There's a lot going on, some pretty serious stuff I have to devote a lot of attention to."

"Care to share?" Marian asked, tilting her glass to her lips and lazily letting some of the wine pour into her mouth.

"No, it's nothing that needs to be discussed right now. But its been a long day," Larry said, moving to stand from his seat. "So I think I'll go upstairs and—"

"Can you hold on a second, Larry, and sit down and talk to me?"

Larry stood over his chair, looking as though he was thinking about rejecting Marian's request, then finally retook his seat. "What is it, Marian?"

As always, she asked herself if she really wanted to have the discussion, but the embarrassment he caused her today in the counselor's office, the heartbreak on their anniversary night, the frustration of waking up in an empty bed, were becoming too much. And then there was the fact that she had a fair amount of liquid courage pumping through her veins. "You've been forgetful lately," Marian said, noticing her words were the slightest bit slurred.

"Marian, I apologized for missing our anniversary and told you I would—"

"I'm not talking about the anniversary!" Marian raised her voice. Only after hearing how loud it echoed did she speak softer. "Last night I asked you in bed if you'd make the appointment at the counselor's office, and you said yes. This morning, I asked you the same thing and you said yes."

"Ugh!" Larry said, slapping a palm to his forehead. He stood from his chair and started around the table to Marian, his arms open as if to hug her.

"No, no, no," Marian said, still holding the almost empty glass in one hand, waving him off with the other. He pulled the seat adjacent to her and sat in it. Marian set the glass down, crossed her arms and lowered her head. She didn't want to look at her husband that moment. She breathed heavily, wiped a tear from her cheek with the cuff of her shirt. "Tell me what you want me to do," she said, her voice barely able to be heard.

"What…what do you mean?" Larry said, reaching out to her, lifting up her chin so that her face could be seen.

"How am I supposed to respond? I love you, but—"

"And I love you, too."

"You aren't acting like it," Marian said. "So am I supposed to worry that this is the end? Is this some phase, some period we're going through, that all couples experience, and I just pretend we're fine and do nothing? Or do I do something else?"

The question was motivated by the thought of Paul. After driving her home from his apartment earlier, they sat parked out front in the circular driveway. Marian didn't get out the car, just sat staring up at the rearview mirror, waiting to see Paul's eyes in it. Finally they appeared.

"Is there anywhere else you want to go?" he said. It was the first words he spoke to her since they had left his place.

"No. You can take personal time till you pick up the kids from school, but…I want to know why you were so angry with me for—"

"I don't wanna talk about that," Paul said. "And I don't have to."

"No. You don't have to, but I still want to know, and…and I think you want to tell me," Marian said, wanting to truly know what was in the man's head.

Paul sighed, shifted uncomfortably in the driver's seat and lowered his eyes from the rearview mirror. "I made a stupid pass at you in the store that day, and you quickly let me know where I stood—where you stood. I got that in my head. I work for you. When I'm driving you, or in your house, you're my boss, and that is what our relationship is," Paul said, his voice lowering to almost a whisper. "But when we were in my place, when you were standing in front of me, looking up at me, all I could imagine doing was taking you, and—"

"Stop it," Marian said, feeling her body start to betray her. She felt flush. A chill passed over her, and she noticed her panties started to moisten. Flustered, she said, "Let's just not talk about it anymore, okay, because what you have in your head is correct, Paul. I am your boss, you do work for me, and that is our relationship." Marian pushed open her door, but before getting out, she said, "And I will never go to your place again."

117

"Marian, I said what do you mean by that?" Larry asked, pulling Marian from her thought. She looked up at Larry. He appeared threatened by her asking if she was expected to do something else.

"Do you want this marriage?" Marian asked, getting to the point.

"What kind of question is that?" Larry said. "You're asking me that with everything that's going on with the church losing money, folks trying to stop me from getting the new church built, and—"

"I know, I know, Larry, and I understand, but I asked you a question. Do you want this marriage?"

"Yes," he said, not waiting a second to give his answer. "Yes, I want it."

Marian exhaled heavily. "Then act like it," she said. She stood from the table and slowly, carefully, made her way to the stairway that led to their bedroom.

28

Robby lay in bed staring through the dark room, still finding it hard to believe the filthy, malnourished young man who walked up to him today, wearing boots and a winter coat in the middle of spring was his one-time best friend Urail.

"Urail?" Robby said, almost dropping his box he was so shocked. He set it down, threw himself into Urail and hugged him. Urail smelled awful and felt as though, under that coat, he was nothing more than skin and bones. Robby stood back, took a long look at him, and had to force himself to smile for fear of crying over of how bad Urail looked. "What's up?" Robby said. "When you come back from Chicago?"

"Chicago?" Urail said. "Never been to Chicago. I always been here. I never been to Chicago."

"Never mind," Robby said. "Looks like you could eat something. You want something to—"

"Burger King," Urail said, smiling.

Twenty minutes later, Robby sat across the table, watching Urail devour his Whopper with cheese, then stare hungrily at Robby's uneaten burger.

"Go ahead," Robby said, pushing his tray toward his friend, having no idea of what could've happened to him to have him looking like that.

Growing up, Van and Urail were Robby's best friends. They went to grade school, middle and high school together. Van was emotional, Robby tough, and Urail, although so hard for Robby to believe at that moment, was the smart one. Urail made A and B grades while Robby scored Ds. The lower marks were something Robby had been just willing to live with, but Urail pushed him to expect more from himself.

"You can do better than that. You making it harder than it has to be. Here," Urail would say, grabbing the pencil from Robby, then showing him how to work a math equation, or punctuate a sentence, or diagram a chart. Urail helped Robby with practically every subject; he was the only reason Robby passed from one grade to the next.

In return, Robby warded off the kids who picked on and bullied Urail because he was a nerd, spoke proper and always had his head in a book. Robby saw Urail as a little brother. He only wanted the best for him and would do anything to make sure no harm ever came to him. But when Robby looked across the Burger King table at his friend, he felt he had failed him.

Robby had taken Urail home, told him he was staying there the night, and made up the living room sofa for him to sleep on. Urail stood by the sofa, smiling excitedly, like a kid at a slumber party.

"Good to see you, Robby. Been wanting to see you. It's good, but when we gonna talk about Bishop?" Urail said.

"It's good to see you, too, Urail," Robby said, fluffing a pillow and setting it on the head of the sofa. "Get some sleep tonight, and maybe we can talk about him tomorrow."

An hour later, Robby lay awake in bed, staring toward the door, angry for so easily allowing his friendship with Urail and Van to dissolve. They all had been members of Bishop Lakes Boy's Ministry. They had all been abused and told to leave when they turned eighteen years old. Because of the shame Robby knew they all felt, they stopped calling and hanging out with each other. That made sense to Robby for a month, until he started missing his friends too much to stay away.

The next day Robby went by the apartment where Van lived with his mother at the time. When Van opened the door and saw Robby, he looked disappointed.

"What do you want, man?" Van asked, closing the door some, as if Robby was a stranger attempting to break in.

"Haven't seen you in a like a month, dude. Was wondering if you…I don't know…wanted to hang out, grab something to eat or something?"

"You know, maybe we shouldn't do that anymore. I'm really kinda busy with—"

"With what, Van?" Robby said, already knowing the excuse he'd be given. "We've all been through it, okay. He did it to all of us. What good does it do us not being friends anymore?"

"I don't know what you're talking about, Robby. Just don't come by here no more," Van said, quickly closing the door.

"Van!" Robby said, banging on the door after it was closed. "C'mon, you were my best friend!"

Robby tried reconnecting with Van several times after that. Van wasn't hearing it, and Robby wasn't the type to force himself on someone who didn't want to be bothered.

A day later, Robby had gone by Urail's mother's house. The security gate opened and Urail's mother, a heavyset woman who always wore shiny black wigs and heavy makeup stood in the doorway.

"Hey Ms. Parker, Urail around?"

Ms. Parker frowned, looked at Robby as though, in all the years Robby and Urail were best friends, she was never able to stand him;

Robby knew that wasn't the case. She had always been friendly and overly sweet to Robby until that moment.

"Urail don't live here anymore. He went to Chicago to live with his uncle," Ms. Parker said.

Robby couldn't believe it. "Are you sure? I'm mean, he didn't call me, or—"

"What do mean, am I sure? I'm his mother! He's in Chicago, so ain't no reason in you coming by here asking for him no more. Goodbye Robby," Ms. Parker said, slamming the security gate in his face.

Now, lying in his bed, Robby asked why Urail's mother would lie like that. Disturbed by the thought, needing to know the answer, Robby climbed out of bed, hoping that maybe Urail was still awake. He stepped into the living room to check and was surprised to see that Urail had taken the pillow and blanket from the sofa, covered himself and had curled up in a corner of the room, where he slept heavily.

The TV was on the news, airing a story that froze and frightened Robby.

29

It was 11 p.m. and Van lay in bed wearing nothing but boxer shorts as he stared up at the faint light the portable TV cast on the ceiling. The drone of a box fan stuck in the window had not put him to sleep as he had hoped. But he was fortunate. The job tip from the strange man that came by the apartment the other day was real. Van had done as he was told and gone to the address on the card. He had to answer a few questions posed by a burly, pink-faced man, the last of which was, "Are you strong? You a hard worker?"

"Yes, sir. I sure am," Van said, still believing someone was playing some kind of joke on him.

The man walked from around his desk, offered a meaty hand to Van, and said, "Good! You're hired. We got some forms for you to fill out, but you start today."

It was a gift. He was in no way deserving, but it was a gift and he was thankful. God is good, he thought.

He worked the hours then rushed home to tell his wife the good news. She jumped in his arms, screamed in his ear and kissed him all over his face. He had never seen Sierra so happy or proud of him in his life.

She lay beside him now, naked, her warm hand brushing up against his thigh. She had roughly an hour before she was to be at work, and Van sensed she wanted sex.

She rolled on her side, facing him. He felt her warm breath on the side of his face. "You up, baby?" she asked.

He closed his eyes and didn't answer.

He felt her moving, then felt her hand slide down the front of his shorts, her wet tongue slipping into his ear. "Sierra no," Van said, grabbing her wrist. "We gonna wake up the baby."

"No we won't," she said, kissing his neck as she tugged softly on his penis. "We'll be quiet." She rolled up on a knee, pressed her lips to his.

Van let his wife's tongue into his mouth, hoping that she could trigger something in him that would allow him to please her. She was hot, excited, and was up straddling his leg, rubbing her clit on his knee till she readied him. But that wasn't happening. His penis was flaccid. He shut his eyes, trying to fight back the horrible things he thought and felt about himself: that he was worthless, a punk, a sissy and a loser, who could not take care of his family or satisfy his wife in bed.

He whipped his head back and forth across his pillow, trying not to cry out, although a tear had escaped his eye. He felt Sierra pulling his boxers down past his hips. All he wanted to do was please her, show her that he loved her, show himself that he was a man.

Sierra lowered herself to Van's pelvis and was kissing his navel.

He felt her warm mouth around him, her tongue massaging his limp penis as she kneaded his testicles in her hands. And all the while, he hated himself, condemned himself, because just the other night he had been erect for Cashmere in that bathroom stall. He could be a man for some freak with pressed hair and fake contacts, but could not please his wife when all she wanted to do was make love to him.

"No Sierra, stop!"

"Baby, I'm gonna do this. It's all right."

"No!" Van said, pushing his wife so hard, she rolled over onto her back, almost falling off the bed. "It's not all right!" Van yelled. He was sitting up, sweat coating his forehead, dripping down his face.

Sierra stared silently at him by the light of the TV. "You don't love me anymore?"

Van shook his head, feeling more shame there in her presence than he ever had. "I do. I love you so much. If you only knew. I just…" And before he could say another word, something on the TV caught his attention. His eyes went wide, and he lunged forward in bed, slapping the blanket, searching for the remote.

"What are you doing?" Sierra said.

"Where's the remote? Turn that up!"

The local news was on. A female reporter stood in front of Holy Sweet Spirit church. A banner on the screen read, "Local bishop accused of molestation."

Sierra dug under the blankets, produced the remote then thumbed up the volume.

"…and earlier today, molestation charges were filed against Bishop Larry Lakes of Holy Sweet Spirit church. We were unable to reach him for comment, but will update you with more details as they come in. Jovita Moore, Channel Two Action News."

On his hands and knees, Van was frozen, staring at the TV.

Sierra looked at him strangely. "Why did you have to hear that?"

Van shook his head and was about to speak, when his cell phone rang. He turned startled toward the milk crate that doubled as a nightstand. It rang a second time.

"Aren't you going to get it?" Sierra said.

He grabbed the phone, hit the ANSWER button and pressed it to his ear. "Hello."

"Van, turn to the Channel Two news."

Van hadn't spoken to the person on the other end of his phone in more than three years, but instantly, he recognized his voice.

"It's on," Van said.

"Did you see it?"

"Yeah, Robby. I saw it."

30

"You should go to jail for this," Mr. Burns had said to Larry ten years ago.

The man was Larry's boss at the used car lot where Larry worked. Mr. Burns had called Larry into his tiny office, closed the door and sat down while Larry stood, knowing why he was there, but knowing the old man had no proof of what he was about to charge him with.

"Tell me how you did it," Mr. Burns said, a scowl on his face, like he couldn't stand the sight of Larry, even though he had praised Larry for the two years he had worked there, calling him his best salesman.

"How I did what, Mr. Burns?"

"Sold cars off my lot without me knowing, pocketing the money for yourself."

"I've never done that. You have proof I did that?" Larry was very careful. He knew the crime of selling the lowest cost cars to his people in the hood and keeping the money would get back to him, so he was very careful to erase any record of the sold cars' existence.

Mr. Burns chuckled sadly and shook his head. "You were the most charismatic, resourceful salesman I ever had. You can sell a car to a man with no arms and no legs, but...but you're a fucking thief, Larry."

"You have no right to call me that if you can't prove it."

"You're right," Mr. Burns said, standing and walking around his desk to his office door. "But I have a right to fire you. Get your ass out of my building. If I ever see you again, I'll make up the proof I need to see you go to jail."

Larry's phone vibrated on his nightstand, snatching him out of his dream. He slammed a hand over the phone before it woke Marian, then brought it to his ear. "Hello," he said, his voice groggy.

"The bitch did it, Bishop!" Tyrell Suggs said. "She went and did it."

"Did what?" Larry said, turning in the dark to make sure that Marian was indeed asleep. By the tone in Tyrell Suggs's voice, the news Larry was about to receive was grave, so he was already pulling himself out of bed. He walked out to the hallway.

"She went to the news people."

"What? How do you know that?"

"It was just on the news. You ain't see?"

Larry felt as though his heart stopped. He turned back to face the bedroom door panicking, wondering if Marian might have been up long enough to see the news, then quickly went to sleep without telling him. But how could that have happened? He speculated about the tens of thousand of people—many of those being the members of his church. What were they thinking that moment?

His breaths came quickly and he felt dizzy. Larry threw out a hand; it landed against a wall and steadied him.

"Bishop, you there?" Tyrell Suggs asked.

"Yeah, yeah," I'm here," Larry said, looking down at the palm full of sweat he pulled from his brow.

"What do you want me to do?"

Larry exhaled deeply, tried his best to gain some form of composure. He had to think right now. "It's too late for you to call anybody, but keep on watching the news. See what they're saying about me. Be here at six o'clock so we can get on this."

"Bishop, you okay?"

"Yeah, I'll be fine. There's just something I have to take care of right now." Larry hung up the phone then walked back into his bedroom. He sat on his wife's side of the bed, just beside her.

There couldn't have been a worse time for this to come out. Just this evening at dinner, Marian questioned him as to whether he wanted to continue in their marriage. After hearing what he was being accused of and the fact that it had gone public, he wondered if Marian would now consider leaving.

He pressed a hand on her shoulder, shook her gently till she awakened.

Her voice low and still filled with sleep, Marian said, "Larry is…is everything all right?"

"I need for you to wake up, Marian."

"Is everything all right?" Marian said, more alert, concern in her voice.

"I need for you to sit up in bed."

"What? What is it?" she said, doing what she was told. "You're starting to worry me."

Larry took his wife's hand then said, "I'm going to turn on the light here, because I need to see you and I need for you to see me when I tell you this."

31

Marian was only twenty-eight when she met Larry at a fundraising ball for a local politician in downtown Atlanta. He approached her very confidently, holding two glasses of champagne. He smiled and held out a glass for her. "Something told me you were thirsty so I brought one for you."

Marian smiled a little and took the glass even though she believed his come-on line was cheesy, as was his cheap suit.

"From now on if there's anything you need I want to be the one to get it for you," the man said, later introducing himself as Larry Lakes. He told her he sold used cars, but that he was aspiring toward much greater things—maybe go back to school—he wasn't sure at that time.

She had tried shaking Used Car Salesman Larry Lakes more than once that night, but he stuck with her, wouldn't let her out of his sight, constantly making his argument as to why she should allow him to take her out sometime, let him get to know her, and find out what a great guy he was.

By the end of the evening, he had grown on her a little, so Marian granted his wish. They went on two dates. She found him charming, confident, and funny; he seemed to know exactly what he wanted—Marian.

On the third date, she told Larry he would have to meet her father first, before taking her out.

Marian waited nervously in the living room, pacing the floor, while Larry spoke to her father in his home study. She stood up when she heard the doors open. Her father, who owned a very lucrative shipping company walked out of the office, shaking Larry's hand and laughing.

He slapped Larry on the back and told him he could step outside to wait for Marian by the car. He wanted to speak to his daughter before they left.

Larry kissed Marian's cheek then walked out the door. Marian turned to her father, beaming, so glad her dad approved of the man she was growing more and more fond of.

"I don't like him, Marian," her father said. "There's something about him…smiling, glad handing—he seems dirty to me, like he's hiding something. And whatever it is, I don't want you anywhere near it."

"I don't agree, Daddy. He's outgoing and happy, and…everyone's not brooding like you."

Marian's father rubbed the gray stubble on his face. "Fine. Go out with him this last time, but at the end of the date, tell him you can't see him anymore."

"No, Daddy. I like him. You're not the one who has to date him. I can do what I want. I'm not you're little girl anymore."

Her father looked saddened by what Marian had told him. He hugged her and gave her a sympathetic smile. "Yes, you can do what you want, but you'll always be my little girl."

Marian closed her eyes against the thought of her late father. She sat by the bedroom window. She had dragged a chair over after waking this morning, had been sitting there, the drape pulled back, a sliver of sunlight cutting across her melancholy face for over an hour. She still wore her nightgown, robe and scarf on her head, unable to do anything

131

more than sit and think about the news her husband had given her last night.

She had sat in shock as Larry told her how he was being accused of molesting Tatiana, who had been a member of the church for the last three years. Marian had known the girl, spoke to her on several occasions, and liked the child a great deal.

Marian's mind raced back to all the interactions she witnessed between Larry and Tatiana, all the conversations they had. Did Marian ever see her husband hug Tatiana or touch her sexually? Did Marian ever see him leaning in, whispering things in her ear? Marian thought she remembered him doing something like that. But at that time, Marian believed the words were harmless—telling her to be good when she got home, or something like that. Now Marian wondered if what he had whispered was how sexy he thought she was, and would she be open for a late night rendezvous?

Shocked by all this last night, the first thing out of Marian's mouth was, "How could you have—"

"I didn't! I told you," Larry said. "She's making it all up, trying to get money from us. You know her father lost his job years ago."

"How do you know she's claiming these things against you?"

"Tyrell Suggs called me. It made the news tonight."

Marian gasped, almost choked. She turned to the TV, expecting it to come on itself, airing the news accusing her husband of molesting the girl. Marian jumped out of bed, hurried to the TV, clicked it on. A commercial ended, and when the news returned, it opened with all the information her husband had just disclosed to her.

She turned to Larry, the remote clutched in her hand. "You're just hearing about this? On the news—this is how you found out?"

Larry dropped his head. "I've known for a week now."

"You've known for a week and you're just telling me this!"

"I was trying to take care of it before it got out, before it could do any harm."

Marian shook her head, feeling betrayed. She clicked off the TV. "Well Larry, you failed. On both counts."

She woke up late this morning. Larry must've turned off the alarm clock, sensing she needed the extra sleep. She did not dream and she was thankful for that. She lay in bed for a while, considered turning on the TV to see what else was being said about her husband, but did not. She turned the ringer on her cell phone off, but couldn't stop the house phone from ringing.

Mrs. Payton, the older woman who cleaned the house and did whatever else needed to be done for the past seven years, knocked softly on Marian's door.

Marian didn't answer.

"Mrs. Lakes," Mrs. Payton said. "There is a phone call for—"

"Turn off the ringers on the home phones, Mrs. Payton," Marian yelled at the door.

"But they say they are from the local news, and—"

"Mrs. Payton, did you hear me?" Marian raised her voice, standing from her chair. "Turn off all the ringers."

She sat down, turned her attention back to her thoughts and continued to stare out the bedroom window. Another knock came.

"Go away."

The door opened. Estelle walked in wearing a tailored pink suit and matching heels. "You look horrible, child."

"Shut the door, Mommy."

Estelle closed the door, walked over, and sat on the windowsill, forcing her daughter to look at her. "I can have Paul carry the kids to school if you like."

"No. I want to go with them just in case...I just need to go."

"I take it you heard what's going on, that's why you're all holed up in this dark room like a vampire."

"Have the kids found out?" Marian asked, brushing hair out of her face.

"I made sure the TVs were off this morning, but they probably will hear every nasty detail the moment they walk on school grounds. You know how kids are."

Marian didn't respond. "Can you get out of my way?" Marian said, pushing a hand into her mother's hip, forcing her off the sill. "You're in my way."

Estelle stood, her hands on her hips, a matching pink purse dangling from her left wrist. She glared at her daughter sadly. "What are you going to do now?"

"What do you mean what am I going to do? Larry told me the girl is lying."

"And you believe him?"

"Of course I do," Marian said, even though last night doubts tried to creep into her head, and this morning, her dead father's voice all but assured her of Larry's guilt. "He's my husband. What else would you have me do?"

"All right, fine. Believe him for now, but you need to get proof."
"Proof? How?"

"I heard about this software that you can put on his—"
"No, Mommy!"

"You can put it on his phone," Estelle said, ignoring her daughter. "Do that, and you can go online to see who he's texting and calling."

"I'm not going to do that!"

"Why not?"

"Why would I?"

Estelle grabbed her daughter tight by the hand. "Because your husband has just been accused of molesting a seventeen-year-old girl. Even if he didn't do it, even if he is innocent, there might be a reason why she felt she could accuse him of such a thing and get away with it. Do you understand what I'm saying? He might not be guilty of that, but he might be guilty of something."

"Fine, fine, I understand," Marian said. She paced away from her mother, hating her for what she was asking Marian to consider.

"I know a man," Estelle said. "He owns a spy shop."

Marian turned back to her mother. "How do you know—"

"Don't you worry about that. I know him. He owns a spy shop and there is software you can put on Larry's phone. Then there is this keystroke software. We put it on his computer, and we'll know all the sites he goes to, and—"

"Mommy," Marian said, walking right up to Estelle, taking her by the arm. "I don't want to do it. Once I do something like that, I'm saying I don't trust my husband anymore."

"Baby," Estelle said, taking her daughter's face in her hands. "Would you rather spy on him and find out he's innocent now, or trust him and find out he's guilty later? Get his phone so I can have this stuff put on, and that way you'll know for sure."

This was all too much for Marian, and she knew if it were just up to her, she wouldn't have the strength to execute this plan. Marian pressed her palms against her mother's, thankful for the warmth and strength she felt in them. She sighed heavily, shut her eyes then said, "Okay Mommy, I'll do it."

32

Van couldn't sleep much last night for thinking about the terrible things he heard on the news, and the phone conversation he had with Robby. Van hadn't spoken to him in so long because he had no desire. Robby was a part of the life that was too painful for Van to think about now. He was trying to forget those years.

"I don't wanna talk," Van said to Robby last night, cupping his hand over the phone. He walked into the bathroom and closed the door so that Sierra wouldn't hear his conversation.

"You see what's on the news?" Robby said. "He's doing it to somebody else. You wanna just do nothing and let that happen?"

"Looks like the girl, whoever she is, is taking care of it."

"Van, Urail showed up at my job, talking about—"

"I don't care what Urail is talking about. Urail is crazy. You know it and I know it, so just…" Van shook his head, wondering why he was even having the conversation. "I don't have nothing else to say, okay Robby. I hope all is good with you, but don't call me anymore."

"Van, we have to do something!"

"Do it yourself." Van ended the call. He flushed the toilet giving him an explanation for sneaking off into the bathroom to begin with, then opened the door and walked back out into the apartment.

"Who was that you were on the phone with?" Sierra asked, sitting up in bed. The look on her face suggested she was preparing herself for bad news.

Van smiled. "Just an old friend."

"What did he want?"

"He wanted to say hi," Van lied, but Robby wanted much more than that. He said they had to do something. Van agreed, something did have to be done, but not what Robby wanted. That was why this morning Van had dialed the phone number he had not dialed in what seemed like forever—the number he used to dial practically every day. When the phone started ringing, he thought to hang up, scared of how the person would react to the call.

"Hello?"

The sound of the voice on the other end of the phone sent a frigid chill over Van's body. He was unable to speak.

"Hello?"

"Sorry to call you," Van tested his voice. "I know you said we shouldn't anymore."

"Van?" Larry asked.

"Yeah. It's me. I'm sorry. I know I shouldn't be—"

"It's okay. I'm sure you have a good reason."

"I need to talk to you…about what's on the news," Van said, the phone pressed hard to the side of his face, his hand trembling around it. When no reply came, Van said, "I just—"

"I'll be in the parking lot of the Varsity in half an hour. You remember the place, right?"

"Yeah, I remember."

Half an hour later, Van parked his Honda in the parking lot of the Varsity burger spot on North Avenue. It was the place Bishop would often take him, Robby and Urail to for lunch.

Looking over his shoulder, feeling very vulnerable, Van walked to the Bentley. He stood nervously outside the door till it was pushed open. He climbed in, lowered himself into the car, feeling a wave of unwelcomed memories, which he quickly fought out of his head. He pulled the door closed and sat as far away from Bishop as possible. He glanced at the man beside him then quickly turned his eyes down. "I didn't wanna call you, but…but I had to ask you something."

Larry chuckled and rested a hand on Van's shoulder like he always used to. "I told you it's okay."

It had been so long since Van was in that car, so long since he had been that close to Bishop that he could not bring himself to look at the man.

"Van, you said you needed to ask me something."

"Did you—" Van started, his eyes still downward.

"What did I teach you?" Bishop said, reaching across the seat, raising Van's chin. "Look people in the eyes when you speak to them. Now ask me."

"Did you do it?" Van said, finally finding the nerve to stare Bishop in the eyes.

"What do you think?"

"I…I don't think you did, because…"

"Because what, son?"

"Because you know the harm it did to us, right? Those things you did to us…we probably never told you, but…to think that you would do that to someone else…" Van said, feeling himself trembling. "I just…"

"Van…son…calm down," Bishop said, holding Van by both shoulders now. He looked seriously into his eyes. "I want you to hear me when I speak these words to you, and I want you to believe them with all your heart. I hurt you boys. I know that now, but that was not my intention. I am truly sorry for the pain it may have caused. I've spoken to the Lord, He has removed all those sinful thoughts and urges from me, and I no longer think or act that way. That's why you are right in knowing I did nothing to that girl, because I don't do that anymore."

"You don't?" Van said, relieved.

"I don't."

Van stared blankly at Bishop for a moment. "You swear?"

Bishop smiled. "I don't have a bible here, but let's pretend I do. I swear on it," he said, raising his right hand.

Van let out a long sigh.

"Good. That is taken care of," Larry said. "Now I really have to be—"

"You sent the man with the job, didn't you?"

"Yes," Larry said, smiling. "Is it working out over there? You like the job?"

Van smiled a little. "I knew it was you. But how did you know I needed work?"

"I know you believed I abandoned you boys, but I keep my eyes on you. I loved you all, and I still do."

Those words pained Van. He winced at the sound of them. "You loved us? You loved us so much that you kicked us out. Loved us so much that you told us never to contact you, to stop coming to church. You told us to stop being with a man that we were told to think of as our father." A single tear raced down Van's cheek.

Bishop appeared saddened. "There is a time for all boys to be men. You had reached that moment. We've been through this. Van, you'll be okay."

"But I'm not! And I won't be!" Van said, striking the seat beside him with a fist. "Do you know what I've been through without you, what I'm going through?"

"I'm sorry," Bishop said. He reached out to Van, tried to hug him. Van beat his hands away, pushed himself even further up against the door of the car, trying to escape Bishop's grasp. "You were my...father. You were a father to all of us. It's what you told us you were. I loved you!" Van sobbed. "And you just left us!"

"I'm sorry. I'm so sorry," Bishop said, taking Van in his arms.

Van tried to deny him, tried not show the weakness that he knew was evident, but he missed him more than even he was aware. Van let himself be held, burying his face into Larry's shoulder, sobbing heavily, wanting never again to release him.

33

Tyrell Suggs smoked a Newport cigarette as he paced the back room floor of Mrs. Earline's restaurant.

A plate of fried chicken and French fries Mrs. Earline prepared for him sat untouched before Larry. He hadn't been able to eat a thing since late last night.

"You gotta call your lawyer," Tyrell Suggs said, pulling the Newport from his lips, blowing smoke into the air. "We gotta tell these people something. They gonna keep on—"

Tyrell Suggs was interrupted by yet another phone call. He pulled his iPhone off his belt clip, glanced at the screen then held it up as though Larry could see it from across the room. "See, it's them again—some reporter or somebody trying to get your side of the story. You gotta tell them something."

Larry didn't respond, just sat at the table, his head in his hand, deep in thought.

This morning he stood over his sleeping wife. She had been tossing and turning all night. He knew she was bothered by what he had told her, and thought of waking Marian, begging her to tell him that she believed him innocent. He extended a hand to her shoulder then pulled back, trusting that she had faith in him.

Without saying goodbye to his children—it was something he realized he had been doing a lot of lately—Larry walked out the front door, climbed into the Bentley and directed Tyrell Suggs to the church, thinking it would be a safe place to come up with the strategy to deal with the mess he was in.

Turning onto Holy Sweet Spirit's street, Tyrell Suggs stopped abruptly.

"What's going on?" Larry said, leaning up in his seat. He didn't have to wait on an answer. Out of the front windshield, he saw the half dozen news vans parked outside his church, the dozen or so reporters and crew holding microphones and cameras, doing on-site broadcasts. He could only imagine what they were saying about him.

Larry struck the seat with a fist beside him hard enough to nearly tear through the leather. "Turn the car around before anyone sees us!"

Earlier this afternoon, after meeting Van and trying to manage the boy in whatever way he could, Larry sat in front of an old, dear friend. His name was Mr. Kendrick. He was a spry sixt-eight years old and one of the first board members of Larry's church. He had been a mentor to Larry, a spiritual father of sorts. He knew all of Larry's secrets and should've known Larry wasn't guilty of what he was being accused of.

Larry sat in the elder's home office after Mr. Kendrick phoned Larry, told him there was something urgent they needed to speak about.

Mr. Kendrick sat behind his desk, his face and head cleanly shaven. He pulled his spectacles from his eyes, shook his head and sighed, disappointed. "I don't know how to say this Larry."

"Then don't," Larry said, not needing to guess what Mr. Kendrick was getting at.

"It's all over the news, and I can't be a part of something like this. You know I have to resign from the—"

"Mr. Kendrick, you know that I didn't do this thing," Larry said.

143

Mr. Kendrick frowned and rubbed a wrinkled hand over his bald skull. "I know you'd have no interest in spending time with that girl. I know that's not where you receive your enjoyment."

Larry took offense to the man's comment with all its implications.

"But innocent or guilty," Mr. Kendrick continued. "This is in the news—it's out. And now there's no telling what else will come out."

"Bishop," Tyrell Suggs called across the back room of Mrs. Earline's. Tyrell Suggs had silenced the phone without taking the call, same as he had done with the last ten calls that came this morning. But Larry heard nothing. He was too deep in thought, further back in his memory, watching from a curb, at the age of seventeen, as his father, wearing dirty jeans and a shirt, shamefully walked up to people at a gas station asking for spare change. Lincoln had been begging for almost an hour. Larry believed he might have collected all of three dollars in that time.

Watching his father degrade himself like that was too much for Larry.

"Please go sit down over there," Larry said, after walking over to Lincoln. "I can do it for a while."

That evening, Larry and Lincoln sat in a truck stop diner, napkins pushed into the collars of their shirts as they hungrily shoveled steak and home-fried potatoes into their mouths.

Halfway through his meal, Lincoln stopped eating to stare across the table at his son. "How did you get so much money?"

"Hunh?" Larry looked up, his cheeks full of food. After only half an hour of begging, Larry had earned fourteen dollars and some change. It was enough to buy two dinner specials and still have money for candy bars on the walk home to the single room in the boarding house they were renting at the time.

"I said—"

"I told them you had cancer, Pops. I pointed to you sitting on the curb, told them you had cancer and you was gonna die in a few weeks and we were hungry."

"Dammit Larry, you ain't supposed to lie to these people. I know we hungry, and we don't have no money, but—"

"But there is no but, Pops. What you just said is all there is. We're hungry and we don't have no money. So our job is to get money so we won't be hungry no more. I'm figuring out its all a game. Everyday, you gotta say what you gotta say and do what you gotta do to get what you want."

"Bishop!" Tyrell Suggs called again, more forcefully.

"Yeah," Larry said, awakened from his thoughts.

"We gotta do something. Can I call your lawyer? I got him right here in my phone, and—"

"No," Larry stood from the table. "I'm not going to use my attorney, because if I call him, that's going to have folks thinking I believe I need him. I don't need him because I'm innocent."

"Are you sure about that?"

"Positive."

"Then we gotta do something. We all locked up in this back room. Feels like we running, and that don't make no sense considering you ain't done nothing wrong."

"You're absolutely right. I haven't done anything wrong. But everyone thinks I have. This is all a game," Larry said. "Everyone thinks I'm the bad bishop: the march, me trying to build my church, my views,

145

my beliefs—people see nothing but the negative. Like I'm the villain. And now this. I'm gonna say what I gotta say, and do what I gotta do." Larry grabbed a chicken leg, tore a bite out of it with his teeth, dropped it back to his plate, then walked around the table.

"And just what does that mean, Bishop," Tyrell Suggs said. His phone started ringing again. He pulled it from his clip, glanced at it. "It's somebody from the news again."

Larry wiped his hands with the nearby paper napkin then reached out for the phone. Tyrell Suggs handed it to Larry.

"This is Bishop Larry Lakes," Larry said, smiling. "How may I help you?"

34

Did he actually do it? The question bounced around in Marian's head for the thousandth time as she stared into the Neiman's dressing room mirror. She stood there, eyes glazed over, in stockings, her bra and panties, thinking about all that was happening.

Had her husband committed the sin he was accused of?

Last night, sitting on the bed beside her, sounding near tears, Larry came off honest enough. He looked like a victim wrongly accused. But this morning when she woke up, he was just gone. He didn't say goodbye to her or the kids and hadn't called her all day.

Marian decided to accompany the kids on the ride to school this morning, just in case there were any questions that needed to be dealt with. Luckily they hadn't heard any news about their father and the charges. It wasn't like they would've been watching the early morning broadcast, but with all the access kids had through the internet and their phones today, Marian wasn't sure.

Marian kissed her children goodbye and almost tearfully she watched them walk away from the car toward the school. She pulled the door closed, slumped in the back seat and instructed Paul to take her home. He nodded from the front seat, silently shifted the car in gear and pulled off. He laughed and joked with the kids as he did every morning, but had not spoken a word to her other than "Good morning".

On the drive to the house, she thought of engaging him in conversation, ask his opinion—he was a man, maybe he would have some insight she didn't. But this was none of his business, so she kicked her legs up onto the seat, folded her arms, tucked her face down, and tried not to think about any of it for a few minutes.

"Mrs. Lakes, what should I do?" Paul asked, ten minutes later. Marian opened her eyes, realizing she must've dozed off. What she saw at the gate in front of her house were three network news vans, cameramen and reporters standing about.

Paul slowed the Lincoln, as not to hit anyone, and the reporters rushed up to the tinted windows of the Town Car.

"What should I do?" Paul asked again.

"Push the damn button to open the gate, and drive in!" Marian said, frustrated and sick of the entire affair. "And if they don't get out the way, run their asses over."

Inside the gate, parked in front of the house, Paul walked around to open Marian's door. As she climbed out, she stopped, stared Paul in the face. "You know what's going on, don't you?"

He nodded, sadly.

"Did my husband do this thing?" Marian asked. "You're a man. You'd know more than I would."

He did not look at her when he said, "I don't think so, Mrs. Lakes."

"You'd be honest with me, tell me the truth if you think he had, wouldn't you?"

Paul turned his eyes to hers, and with what she felt was complete sincerity said, "Yes I would."

Fighting the urge to turn on the television and check the news, Marian napped as best she could before picking up the kids.

Paul drove her back, but opposed to this morning, when the children laughed and played with Paul, on the ride home, Jabari sat quietly beside Marian, his arms crossed, while Simone sat in her car seat, playing with one of her dolls.

"You okay, son?" Marian said, as the car halted at a stoplight.

The boy didn't answer.

"Jabari," Marian said, placing a hand on his arm. "I asked you are you okay?"

"Why did Daddy do it?" he said, near tears.

Marian looked up, saw Paul's eyes in the rearview mirror, as if to question how she would handle the boy's question.

The rest of the ride home Marian tried to explain to her son that her father did nothing wrong. And that just because he was accused of something, didn't make him guilty.

"All the kids say he messed with Tatiana…did stuff to her." Jabari went on to tell Marian how they made nasty jokes about his father, how they called Jabari a pervert because his father was one.

Marian clenched her teeth, fighting the urge to just scream, angry that she had to defend Larry because he chose not to be there to do so himself.

When they made it home, Marian told Jabari to take Simone into the house and that she'd be along in just a moment. Paul stood by after opening the door for the kids. Marian watched the front door of the house, saw it close after the kids disappeared into it.

She turned to Paul. "The other day, you had something to tell me about my husband."

Paul shook his head. "No I didn't."

"You did. Does it have to do with this thing with the girl?" Marian said.

"Mrs. Lakes, I told you. I had nothing to tell you about your husband. I wouldn't lie to you."

Marian glared into Paul's eyes a moment before saying, "I hope to God you're being honest. If you're not, I'll never trust you with anything again, least of all my children."

35

Sitting in the back seat of the Bentley, Larry glanced down at his watch; it was approaching seven o'clock. The work he had done today, he was sure, had already aired on the early 4:30 news and all the other evening broadcasts.

He had Tyrell Suggs drive him around to all the stations that wanted to interview him. He sat down in front of the cameras with the reporters, took their questions—"Why would Tatiana Benson accuse you of molesting her, of physically assaulting her if it is not true?"

Larry smiled, remained calm and confident and said, "I don't know. I don't want to speculate about her and her family, but I know they were suffering through hard times like so many Americans. I'm sure that might have had something to do with all of this, but I can't be sure. All I know is, I did nothing wrong to that child. She is a member of my church, and for all the boys and girls who are, there is no safer place in the world for them."

"Thank you Bishop Lakes," Monica Kauffman, an older woman with short salt and pepper hair said, shook Larry's hand.

"You're very welcome, Monica," Larry said.

He and Tyrell Suggs left the news station twenty-five minutes ago, and now Larry sat in the back seat of the Bentley on his phone. It had been a hectic day, doing interviews, calling all of the board members of the church, speaking to them individually and letting them know he did not do what he was being accused of. He did not need any more defectors like Mr. Kendrick. His board dismantling did terrible harm to the church, but also to the church's image. If his own people started to jump ship, what would the public and his followers start to think? The last thing he needed were members of the church questioning whether or not they should still attend and still donate. Larry needed money now more than ever.

Larry's phone rang.

Before picking it up, he saw Bishop Ridgeway's name on the screen. Larry thought about not answering, but told himself not speaking to the man would come off as running, as having something to hide.

"Bishop Ridgeway," Larry said, picking up.

Ridgeway didn't answer right away. There was silence then chuckling. "And you wonder why we don't want you building a church in our city."

"You know good and well I didn't do this thing."

"Do I know that, Bishop? If you didn't, that girl wouldn't be all over the news saying you did. It's on right now."

"And I'm all over the news saying I didn't do it."

"I wouldn't have expected anything less, Larry. Doesn't matter," Ridgeway said. "We're not going to let you in our city, and after the truth comes out about this fuck up, no one will want you there anyway. Goodbye, Bishop," Ridgeway said, hanging up the phone.

Not thirty seconds later, Larry was ringing the Union City Mayor's phone. Richard Bonner picked up on the second ring.

"I'm not liking this, Bishop Lakes," Mayor Bonner said without saying hello. "It doesn't look good."

"It's not true."

"It still looks bad. We might have to recon—"

"Did you meet with Shreeva?"

"Well…"

"Mayor, did you meet with her and was she what you expected?"

"More. Much more, and I hope to see her again, but—"

152

"But nothing," Larry said, trying to control an emerging anger he felt might get out of hand if he spoke to this man for too much longer. "We made a deal. I delivered, you benefited, and you still have yet to benefit. It would be bad for your reputation if word got out that you reneged."

"You trying to threaten me?" Mayor Bonner said.

"Not at all. I'm just reminding you that we had an agreement, and I expect you to honor that, Mayor Bonner. Goodbye."

Yes, it had been a long day. Now that it was just about over, Larry needed to do something that would take his mind off all the toiling, something that would give him pleasure.

He picked up his phone and dialed Omar's cell phone. He had been thinking about him all day and wanted to check in on him, see how he was doing.

When Omar picked up, he sounded happy to hear from Larry, something that made Larry feel good after such a trying day. He asked Larry if he wanted to come by his house.

"Come by?" Larry said. "I don't think that would be such a good idea. Isn't your mother there? What would she think?"

"She's still at work. She won't be back for another two hours."

"You sure about that?"

"Yeah," Omar laughed. "It'll be fine."

Larry loved the carefree, innocent tone of the boy's voice. He glanced down at his watch again, determining if he could fit a very short visit in.

"Yeah okay, sure," Larry said. "Text me your address, and I'll be that way in a half an hour or so." He hung up the phone, powered down the privacy glass.

"What's up, Bishop?" Tyrell Suggs said, looking at Larry through his rearview mirror.

"Run by Lenox Mall. I want to pick up something, then we'll make one last stop before taking it home."

Larry waited for the door of the small house in the Washington Park area of town to open up. The neighborhood was sketchy; Larry kept looking over his shoulder at the Bentley parked on this street of dilapidated houses.

When he turned around, the door was open. Omar stood before him wearing jeans, tennis shoes and no shirt. He played high school football and was a perfectly beautiful, muscled specimen of a seventeen-year-old boy. His skin was smooth and blemish free. His shoulders, biceps and abdominal muscles were all very nicely sculptured, and not a strand of hair grew from his bare torso. Larry took the boy in a moment before speaking.

"How are you, Omar?"

Omar smiled, held open the screen door and stepped aside for Larry to enter.

Larry walked into a modestly decorated home. It reminded him of one of the places he and his father rented when he was a child.

"I saw the stuff on the news," Omar said. "Did you do it?"

"No. It's the reason I agreed to come by. I wanted to tell you face to face that I wouldn't do something like that. Do you believe me when I say I had nothing to do with any of that?" Larry asked, not

154

knowing why it was so important that this boy trust him, that this boy not think of him as some sexual predator.

"Yeah," Omar said, looking into Larry's eyes. "I know you wouldn't do nothing like that. I know you wouldn't."

Larry dug out the box from the bag he was holding and presented it to Omar.

The boy eagerly cracked it open. Inside was a beautiful, expensive Swiss watch.

"Wooh!" Omar said, pulling the watch from the casing. "What is it?"

"It's a Tag Heur," Larry said. "Very fine watches. The kind Tiger Woods used to endorse before the fool boy got caught up in all that sex scandal stuff. I had one of my own before I graduated up to Cartier and Rolex."

"Wow! Thank you so much," Omar said, and before Larry could stop him, the boy had thrown his arms around him, was pressing his bare torso to Larry, holding him tight.

Larry stood there, frozen, his arms by his sides, not knowing what to do with his hands. The sides of their faces touched; one of the boy's earlobes grazed Larry's lower lip. Larry's mind went crazy with thoughts he knew he should not have been having.

Omar released Larry and stepped back. "Thanks again!"

Larry forced his attention on the watch and not the boy's beautiful body or the thought of him standing totally naked in front of Larry. "You're welcome, but your mother can't see that. She might start to…just don't let her see it, or tell her I bought it for you. Can that be our little secret?"

Omar smiled, looked down at his new watch then admiringly up at Larry. "Yeah, it'll be our little secret."

36

Van watched as Sierra sat at the folding table, eating the dinner of pork chops, macaroni and cheese and corn on the cob she had made them. It was all food the money from Van's new job provided. He felt proud sitting there. Proud to watch his son sit in his booster chair, eating and laughing, his fingers and face covered in yellow cheese sauce.

"You okay?" Van asked his wife, knowing what her answer would be. It was all over her face.

She nodded and smiled, reached over, squeezed his hand. "Things good with you at work?"

"Yup," Van said, so thankful for Bishop getting him the job, making everything better like he used to do. "I really like it."

"I got some good news, baby," Sierra said, practically trembling in her chair with excitement. "One of the other guards left, so my boss is changing my schedule to days. I'm gonna switch my classes to evenings, so I'll be home with you and Virgil at night. Isn't that great, baby?" She squeezed Van's hand even tighter now.

Van stood, pulled her from her chair, and hugged her tight.

"Its really great news, baby," Van said, kissing her softly on the side of her neck.

"Things are getting better for us Van," Sierra whispered in his ear. He could hear the joy and the relief in her voice. "We're both working now. We'll have extra money and whatever you was thinking about, whatever was always bothering you, you don't have to worry about no more."

"You right, I don't," Van said, gazing into Sierra's eyes.

"I can tell you feeling better. I can just see it. And everything is gonna be all right."

And she was right, Van thought. But it wasn't just because of the new job. It was also because of what Bishop told him earlier today, after releasing him from their embrace.

"Not a day goes by when I don't think about you boys—all of you. I hope you know that," Larry said, looking troubled by regret. "Maybe I shouldn't have just separated from you all like that. You were men, and I was taught that men have to find their own way."

"But you could've still helped us, could've at least still talked to us," Van said, smearing tears from his face. "It doesn't have to be like before. If I could just talk to you when something's on my mind, when I'm having trouble and I don't know the answer to something. It would be nice if I could come to you."

"Is that what you want?" Bishop asked.

Van was surprised that Bishop would actually consider such an arrangement, after he so rudely cast them from the church.

"I miss having you in my life," Van said. "Yeah, that's what I want."

Larry smiled and nodded. "Then that's what we'll do. Whenever something's on your mind again, whenever you want to just talk, give me a call, son."

Van refocused his attention on Sierra, his arms still wrapped around her. "Yeah baby, I'm feeling much better. And everything *is* gonna be just fine."

37

The Bentley sedan pulled alongside the front curb of Larry's church, after coming from Omar's house.

Tyrell Suggs parked then asked, "What you want me to get out of there, Bishop?"

"Don't worry about it. I'll go in," Larry said, happy to no longer see the news crews and their vans parked curbside. "There are a couple of other things I need to check on," Larry said, pulling on the door handle.

"You want me to go in with you? It's getting dark outside. You never know if that crazy boy might be out there lurking again."

Larry smiled, thankful for his old friend. "That's why I hired that guy," Larry said, nodding toward Officer Payton, standing some seventy-five yards away, by the front door of the church. "I'll be fine."

Larry stepped out, closed the door and started toward the church's stairs. Yes, it had been a rough day. It seemed he had to explain himself not only to the reporters, but to almost everyone he knew, everyone he had any association with, except his wife. Marian hadn't called today.

As Larry walked closer toward the church stairs, he heard a car door slam. He paid it no mind. His thoughts were on Marian that moment.

Just two nights ago, she voiced her concern about their marriage and asked him if he still wanted it. The skepticism he felt as she glared at him across the dining room table made him think she didn't believe he still wanted to be married. True or not, it did neither of them any good her questioning him like that.

Then last night came the painful confession of the molestation allegations. She was shaken pretty badly hearing it, but so was he, having to deal with the nonsense. With all that he was going through today, he would've expected Marian to ring him and at least ask how he was faring through it all. But no call came.

Larry walked up to the stairs, was about to climb the first, when out the corner of his eye he saw movement. Suddenly, he heard Tyrell Suggs's loud voice yelling at him. "Bishop, Bishop, look out!"

Larry whipped his head around, looked back toward the car to see Tyrell Suggs running furiously at him, pointing past Larry.

Larry heard loud footsteps—the heavy soles of hard shoes slapping the cement stairs, and when he turned in that direction, he saw Officer Payton, awkwardly running down the stairs.

"Bishop Lakes get out the way!" Officer Payton yelled.

Larry spun in the direction that both Payton and Tyrell Suggs pointed in to see a man walking briskly toward him from across the street. It was too dark to make out who the man was, but what Larry did see was the gun extended out in front of him.

Officer Payton came to a halt, ten feet to Larry's left, bent over, hands on his knees, huffing. Tyrell Suggs stopped at the same distance behind the man with the gun.

"Put the fucking gun down, man!" Tyrell Suggs yelled.

"My little girl," the gunman said, his voice low, but loud enough for all to hear. "You do that to my little girl!"

Finally Larry recognized the man's face. It was Mr. Benson, Tatiana's father. He must've been sitting in his car, waiting, hoping that Larry would come here so that he could confront him.

With both Tyrell Suggs and Officer Payton yelling, Larry turned, raised both his palms and said, "Mr. Benson, I did not do this. I would not do this. I have a daughter of my own. Why would I do something like that?"

But Mr. Benson wasn't there to be reasoned with. Larry saw him take another step closer, putting him on the sidewalk just in front of the church. He raised the gun higher, at the level of Larry's face, squinted an eye as if taking aim.

"Don't do it!" Tyrell Suggs yelled. Don't you—"

"She was my little girl!" Mr. Benson said. "We trusted you and you did those horrible things to her."

"Mr. Benson," Larry said, imagining his wife and his children, standing before his casket, howling, shedding tears, never knowing that when he died he was an innocent man. "I swear to God that—"

"God does not know you, Bishop Lakes, and He will not miss you when you burn in hell!" With that said, Mr. Benson pulled the trigger.

Larry saw the flash of fire pour from the gun. The bullet hit him with the force of a speeding car, slamming him to the ground. The bullet had ripped his flesh and burrowed deep into his body. Larry lay there, eyes wide, whirling about in his head, his left arm and right leg shaking violently.

"The Lord is my shepherd, I shall not…want. He makes me lie down…" Larry mumbled, but could not remember what came next. He stared into the heavens and begged God to spare his life this night.

38

Marian called Paul after trying to find sleep, but failing for two hours.

She told him to drive her to Twist, a trendy restaurant in Buckhead she occasionally visited. She just needed to get out of that house.

In the sparsely populated, dim restaurant, where the techno music was so loud Marian could hardly hear herself think, Paul silently sat beside her, shooing off men who tried to approach.

Attempting to blot any memory of last night and this morning, Marian downed three double vodka gimlets. Her head whirled, and she almost slipped off her stool as she waved down the bartender for another.

Paul was there to scoop her up and not let her make a scene. She heard him tell the bartender that the lady has had enough, and then he called for the check.

She didn't remember every step she took to get there, but she knew Paul was beside her, his arm around her waist, steadying her as she wobbled back to the Town Car.

"Should I take you home?" He asked from the front seat.

"No," Marian said, leaning up on the seat, only a mild slur in her speech when she said, "Take me to Neiman. I need to go shopping and spend lots of money."

Marian had been shopping for not quite an hour and had sobered up enough to try on dresses by herself. She had half a dozen garments hanging in the dressing room, each one cost more than a thousand dollars.

A knock came at the room door. "Yeah?"

"I got the dress you wanted in a size four," Paul said.

On the drive over, Marian sat, her head back, wearing her dark Versace glasses. Paul didn't speak or ask any questions about the accusations made against her husband. All evening he had behaved like a perfect gentleman, treating her in an almost formal manner. She wondered what happened to the man who had kidnapped her and her children and taken them for ice cream, or the man who had made the pass at her in the middle of the department store. Yes, she had scolded Paul for both those actions, and had reiterated the fact that she was his boss and nothing else, but in light of what was happening now, Marian felt she needed that little bit of attention she had been used to getting from him. She didn't know if it was because her husband hadn't made love to her in months, hadn't kissed her passionately, hadn't even been affectionate with her, or if it was the fact that he might have betrayed her with a little girl. Either way, Marian would've felt better about herself knowing another man had shown some attraction to her—letting her know that Larry wasn't neglecting her because she had become hard on the eyes.

Standing outside the dressing room door, Paul said, "You want me to hand you the dress over the door?"

Marian turned back toward the mirror then dug in her purse that hung on a hook to her left. She fished out her phone to see that Larry still hadn't called. She dropped the phone back in her bag, then peeled off her stockings and tossed them to a corner of the dressing room. "No," she said, reaching around her back and unclasping her bra, tossing that as well. She felt the cool air chill her skin. Her nipples immediately grew hard.

163

"Open the door and hand it to me," Marian said, sliding the tiny button to unlock the door. She stepped back and watched as the knob turned. When the door opened, she saw the surprise on Paul's face. He gasped, but maintained control saying, "Where you want me to leave it?"

Marian took a moment to answer. She stared him in the face, wanting to see how long it would take for his eyes to drop and gaze at her breasts.

"Don't leave. Close the door," she said, taking the dress from the hanger. "I want your opinion."

Paul did as he was told, closing them into the very small space. Marian turned her back to Paul, almost brushing her behind against his crotch.

She bent over to step into the dress, and looked into the mirror to see that Paul's eyes were locked on her behind. His penis had grown erect and was pressing an imprint against his trousers. Judging by what Marian saw, he was much larger than she had imagined in the dreams she had of him.

"Zip me up, please."

Paul reached over and zipped the dress closed.

She turned to him. "What do you think?"

"It's...it's nice."

"That's it?"

"I mean, what else do you want me to say?"

Marian reached out, wrapped her hand around his manhood, gently squeezed it, never taking her eyes from him his. He maintained complete composure, but when she squeezed him a bit harder, she saw his eyelids lower and felt him shudder. "Judging by this thing growing in your slacks, I would've thought more than just nice," Marian said, releasing him.

Embarrassed, Paul sunk a hand into his pocket and re-positioned himself. "Sorry about that."

"Don't be," Marian said, accomplishing her goal for the evening. "Now unzip me and get out."

After the door was closed, Marian sat on the dressing room bench, blushing. She closed her eyes. An image flashed through her head of her in that tiny room, on her knees in front of Paul, slowly unzipping his fly.

She shook her head, opened her eyes and said, "No!" She fanned herself with a hand, aware that she would definitely have to keep her distance from him.

Marian stood, pushed the dress down off her hips when her cell phone rang. She grabbed it out of her purse, answered it without looking, hoping it was her husband.

"Mrs. Lakes?" an unrecognizable voice asked.

"Yes, this is Mrs. Lakes."

"We need you to come to Piedmont Hospital. Your husband has been shot."

39

Marian hurried into the emergency room, tears streaming down her face. She scanned the area, breathing heavy. When she saw her mother and her children, she ran to them.

"What happened? Oh God, what happened to him?"

"Calm down," Estelle said, hugging Marian.

Marian felt her children by her side, hugging her waist. She reached down and pressed their heads closer to her.

"The father of the girl accusing Larry of you know what, shot him," Estelle said.

"My God, is he all right?" Marian cried, smearing tears from her cheeks. "Is he okay?"

"The doctor came out a little while ago and said he would be fine. He was shot in the shoulder. He said they would take out the bullet, stitch him up and he would be fine."

Marian breathed a sigh of relief. She kneeled down to her children, took them both in her arms, kissed their faces and said, "Thank God, oh thank God."

The doctors did as they said, removed the bullet, stitched and bandaged Larry up. They had given him a room and planned to keep him overnight for observation.

Marian had brought the kids in to see him. They hugged him very gently, kissed his face, told him how much they loved him, and made sure he would be okay. Marian ushered them out so Larry could get some much-needed rest.

Now she sat alone with him, a tissue pressed to her face, feeling terribly guilty about where she had been, what she was doing and thinking at the time her husband had been gunned down.

Larry opened a hand that lay on the sheets of his bed. Marian took it, raised it to her lips and kissed it.

"I'm so sorry," she said. "You could've been killed."

"I wasn't. He was watching over me. I'll be fine," Larry said, his voice groggy from pain medication. "They have to come harder than that to take me down."

"What happened to him?"

"The girl's father?" Larry said, turning a little in bed to face Marian, wincing due to the pain it caused him. "He really thought I did it, so...he did something about it. I believe it's what any father would've done."

"It was still wrong. Especially because you're innocent." Marian sidled up closer to her husband. "I'm so glad you're all right. The thought of ever losing you is—"

"I told you," Larry said, trying to smile, but appearing too tired. "Stop that. That ain't ever going to happen. Now it's late. I feel these drugs starting to work, and I don't want to be rude and fall asleep on you, baby."

"Okay, I'll let you rest," Marian said, standing and leaning over her husband. She kissed him softly on the lips. "I love you."

"I love you, too," Larry said.

When Marian stepped out of the hospital room, Estelle was waiting just down the hall, holding a clear, plastic bag.

"How is he?" Estelle asked.

"He's going to be fine," Marian said, dabbing at her eyes with her tissue. She forced herself to smile. "Yeah, he's going to be just fine. Where are the kids?"

"I left them down the hall in the waiting room. They're watching TV."

"Okay. I think I need to go and explain this just a little more to them."

"Probably so," Estelle said. "But first I want to know are we still okay with what we talked about the other day? You know, the software."

"Really, Mommy? My husband has just been shot, and you still want to do this?"

"This is the time. He's here, away from the house till tomorrow."

"But—"

"But nothing," Estelle said, stepping closer to her daughter, looking over her shoulder before she spoke. "Yes, the girl could be lying, but if she is, they're doing a hell of lot: hiring an attorney, going on the news, and trying to kill your husband just to make it look like the truth." Estelle grabbed Marian by the shoulder. "We need to do this to know for ourselves. Let me. The nurse gave me all of Larry's belongings. They're all in this bag, including his phone. All you have to do is give me permission."

Marian thought about everything her mother said. Yes, Marian believed Larry was innocent, but Mr. Benson thought he was guilty—so guilty that he took a gun and tried to murder him. For her sake, her children's, and the Benson family's, Marian had to find out if there was any truth to anything Tatiana said.

"Fine, Mommy," Marian said. "Do what you have to do."

40

The next morning, Marian brushed her hair after applying lipstick. Larry had called an hour ago and said the doctors were ready to release him. She glanced in the bathroom mirror one last time before leaving for the hospital to pick up her husband.

Marian set the brush back in the bathroom drawer, and closed it. She was still sick with guilt, could barely stand the sight of herself for playing games with another man while her husband could've been killed.

She cried herself to sleep last night, pained so much by what would've happened if Larry had been fatally wounded. The only way she was able to get past the guilt and get to sleep was to acknowledge that nothing really happened in that dressing room with Paul other than a little foolish fondling.

Marian grabbed her purse and stepped out the bedroom. Estelle stood by the door. "Hey Mommy, did Paul get the kids to school okay?" Marian asked.

"Yes, but Jabari didn't want to go. He kept saying the kids there would make fun of him again. Maybe we should've just kept him out, because if anyone says another word to my grandbaby, they gonna have to arrest an old lady for child abuse."

"Calm down, Mommy. I told Jabari at breakfast this morning that he just has to ignore them. He'll be fine. I'm going to pick up Larry," Marian said, leaning in, giving Estelle a kiss on the cheek. "We'll see you when—"

"Won't he need his cell?" Estelle said, holding Larry's phone out to Marian.

Marian looked at it like it was covered with poisonous barbs.

"Take it. He's going to ask for it."

Marian took the phone. "Did you…"

"I did. Last night. All you have to do is go on-line and—"

"Mommy, I've changed my mind."

"No. You're going to do this!"

"Larry didn't do anything wrong!"

"Tell me you know that for sure and you're not just feeling sorry for him because he got shot."

Marian stared, unblinking at her mother.

"Well, are you sure?"

"Fine." Marian stepped past her mother, about to start down the hall.

"And the guy should be here any minute to install the stuff on Larry's computer. It shouldn't take him any longer than twenty minutes. Your husband's office is open, right?"

Marian's back was to her mother. She didn't turn around, just frowned and shook her head when she said, "Yes. It's open."

"You want me to have him put in some tiny microphones and cameras, too? He got all that stuff."

Marian spun. "No, Mommy! I think this is going far enough. Don't you?"

Half an hour later, Paul pulled the Lincoln to a stop in front of the hospital's entrance. He had been quiet riding over. It was exactly what Marian needed. She didn't feel like engaging in questions about what happened yesterday and what the hell it all meant.

She gathered her purse from the floor and prepared to step out of the car.

"Can you hold it a minute?" Paul asked.

"What is it?" Marian snapped, not taking her hand off of the door handle, or turning to meet his eyes in the rearview mirror.

"Yesterday, in the dressing room. What was that?"

Marian sighed and turned her eyes on him. "I don't know if you watched the news, but if you had, you would know that my husband was shot by the father of the girl who's falsely accusing him of molesting her."

"I know about that," Paul said, turning to look over the seat at Marian.

"My husband could've been killed, and you're asking me—"

"But your husband wasn't killed. On the news they say he's going to be fine. And maybe someone wouldn't have been trying to kill him if—"

"If what?" Marian said outraged that her hired help actually had the nerve to say something negative about the man who hired him.

Reluctantly, Paul said, "If...if he was a better man."

"A better man? What in the hell makes you say that?"

Paul turned away, looking anguished by the thoughts in his head. He looked like he knew something, like he had something he wanted to get off his chest. When he turned back, he said, "Maybe he's not..."

"Not what, Paul? If there's something you have to say, say it!"

Paul shook his head. "Nothing. I just wanna know what happened in that dressing room—what's happening with us?"

"Nothing happened. You hear me? Nothing happened!" Marian said firmly, slipping on her sunglasses and pushing open the door, filling

171

the car's cabin with bright sunlight. "And I need for you to understand that absolutely nothing *is* happening with us and nothing ever will!"

41

Larry stood in the middle of his hospital room wearing the slacks he had been brought here in and a crisp white dress shirt he had Tyrell Suggs buy for him.

Larry's left arm hung immobilized in a sling to avoid him aggravating the injury.

The doctor told him he might feel some discomfort over the next couple of days, but that there was no bone or arterial involvement, and that he should be just fine. That was good news, but it couldn't compare to what he was staring at on the morning newscast that moment.

Tyrell Suggs stood beside Larry wearing another sharp suit and shiny, pointy-toed white shoes, his arms crossed. "See, see, I told you that girl was lying," Tyrell Suggs said.

Larry continued listening to the broadcast, a smile on his face.

"…in a strange turn of events, the girl accusing head of Holy Sweet Spirit church, Bishop Larry Lakes of molestation recanted those accusations after her father shot the controversial church leader last night."

Footage of Tatiana giving a statement was shown on the screen. "I'm sorry," the girl said, her cheeks wet with tears. "I made the whole thing up. Bishop Lakes has lots of money, and I thought I could get some for my parents. We just needed money. I didn't know Dad would shoot him."

The Tatiana footage stopped, and the newscaster appeared back on screen, shaking her head, pausing thoughtfully as if wanting to make a personal comment then said, "We have not had an opportunity to speak with Bishop Lakes who is expected to make a full recovery from his injuries. Reporting live—"

Larry muted the TV.

"That's a good thing, Bishop. Congratulations!" Tyrell Suggs said, patting Larry on his uninjured shoulder. "What happens next? We still have to get you to the police station so you can press charges against that girl's crazy father."

Larry paced away from Tyrell Suggs, stopping to stare out the windows. "I want to talk to the Benson attorney first. I'm not certain if—" Larry was interrupted by the ringing of his hospital room phone. Tyrell Suggs picked it up and held the receiver out for Larry to take it.

"This is Bishop Lakes."

It was the Benson attorney. "First, let me apologize for the false accusations made against you," Attorney Michaels said. "I truly believed what Tatiana told me when she said—"

"I told you what she said wasn't true."

"I know, Bishop Lakes, but—"

"But you believed a child over me."

"That child is my client. That's what I get paid for. In this case, unfortunately, my client lied, and I am deeply sorry."

Larry took a deep breath, relaxed some, telling himself Attorney Michaels wasn't to blame for all that happened. "Fine. I accept your apology. But just like you went in front of the camera when you accused me of that horrible act, I need for you to go right back there so all the world can see that you made a mistake."

"I planned to do just that later this afternoon."

"Good."

"But that is not the only reason I'm calling, Bishop. As you know, the hardship the Benson family faces right now is what motivated Tatiana's lie in the first place. Her father hasn't worked in years, but he's looking. If he's sent to prison, they'll be far worse off now than—"

"Ms. Michaels," Larry said, looking up at Tyrell Suggs. "Are you asking me not to press charges against Mr. Benson? Is that what you're getting at?"

"Oh no she's not!" Tyrell Suggs said, walking over quickly and standing in front of Larry.

Larry pulled the phone from his face, cupped a hand over the receiver. "Do you believe this woman?"

"Tell her she knows where she can go," Tyrell Suggs said.

Larry placed the phone back to his ear and heard Ms. Michaels say, "Yes, that's exactly what I'm getting at. If you would just—"

"Ms. Michaels, hold on a moment, please," Larry said, covering the mouthpiece again, reconsidering what was just asked of him. Larry envisioned the sequence of events for both scenarios—if he were to press charges and if he was not—then raised the phone back to his ear. "Fine, Ms. Michaels, fine. I won't press charges."

"What?" Tyrell Suggs said, his voice quieted in respect for the phone call.

"I won't press charges against Mr. Benson, but there will be conditions," Larry said.

42

Van stopped the car in front of his apartment building after another long, satisfying day of work.

Van had seen on the news that Bishop had been shot and he thanked God that he would be okay. At least that's what was reported on the news. Van had tried ringing his phone, but the calls went straight to voicemail.

Van climbed out of his car, reached back in to retrieve his book bag, when he was startled by Robby's Jeep. It raced up beside Van, almost tearing the door off the little Honda.

"We need to talk man," Robby said, leaning an elbow out the window. Urail sat in the passenger seat still wearing his winter coat. He looked straight ahead, not acknowledging Van.

"Did you see that news?" Van said. "There's no need for us to—"

"Get in the Jeep, Van," Robby said. "I said we need to talk."

"But he's innocent."

"Get in the fucking Jeep before I have to get out and make you get in," Robby threatened.

The three boys ended up at a small bar in the hood. Four small tables and several mismatched chairs sat empty in the center of the establishment's floor. The door was propped open to let a cool breeze in, as an old Whitney Houston song played from an outdated boom box behind the bar.

Robby and Urail drank from beers a heavyset bartender had given them.

Van held his in both hands but hadn't taken a drink. "I don't know why we even here."

"Because Urail thinks it's time for Bishop to fess up to what he did to us," Robby said.

"That's what Urail thinks, huh? No offense, Urail," Van said to him. "But he sleeps on my floor sometimes, and he's wearing a winter coat, and its eighty degrees outside, so why should we do anything about what Urail thinks?"

"Because it's true," Urail said, sounding hurt by Van's comments.

"Why do you think that, Urail?" Van said.

Urail muttered something under his voice.

Van was up off his barstool. He walked around Robby, angrily grabbing Urail by the arm, jerking him. "Why is it all of a sudden time? It's been three years. Why wasn't it time a year ago? Two years ago? Why now, Urail?"

"Because it is!" Urail yelled.

"You're fucking crazy, and you don't know what you're talking about!" Van yelled louder, shaking him again.

"Hey, hey, hey!" Robby said, pulling Van's hands off of Urail. "You acting like he did something wrong. He's just trying to fix this."

"There ain't no fixing this," Van said. "It happened, and all we can do is ignore it and try to deal with it, but there ain't no fucking fixing it. Just let it be," Van said, only momentarily thinking of telling them of his conversation with Bishop—the arrangement he now had. Maybe Robby and Urail would stop with all the foolish talk of going after him if

177

they knew they could have him back in their lives. But Van realized just by looking and listening to the two, that was not what they wanted.

"So you cool with the way things are?" Robby said. "You cool with letting him get away with what he did to us? You cool with just trying to deal with it?"

"I ain't crazy enough to think that something else can be done," Van said. "So yeah, I'm cool with it."

"Really," Robby said. "So you ain't having no nightmares? No fucked up feelings, wondering why you? No sick-ass flashbacks of what he used to do to us?"

Van didn't answer.

"And how's your family dealing with it? Urail told me you got a wife and kid now."

"Leave my family out of this," Van grunted.

"You tell her yet?" Robby said.

"No," Urail said.

"I said, leave them out of this," Van said, stepping in Robby's face.

"Naw, man," Robby said. "You dealing with this. All is good with you. It should be no problem your wife knowing her husband was some old man's bitch."

Van reared back, threw a fist at Robby. Robby blocked it with a forearm, threw a punch of his own, hit Van across the chin, dropping him to the barroom floor.

"Hey, ain't gonna be no fighting in here!" The bartender said, appearing out of a back room behind the bar.

"Everything is fine, Sam," Robby said to the man, reaching down, helping Van off the floor. "Now answer my question," Robby

178

said, in Van's face, holding him by the front of his shirt. "Ever thought about taking pills or sucking on the barrel of a gun and just ending it to make all the shit in your head stop?"

Van didn't answer, just stared, seething, through narrowed eyes at his one-time friend.

"Answer the fucking question!" Robby yelled.

"Yes, okay! Yes! But we can't do anything about it. You see what happened to the girl on the news. How we gonna look saying this stuff after what the girl just said about him? We gonna look just as stupid as she looked. Bishop's gonna deny everything, and we're gonna look like fools."

"Then we don't give him the option to deny it," Robby said, releasing Van. "We get proof on his ass and make this shit official."

43

Marian sat at the dining room table, smiling at Larry. He sat across from her, still wearing his sling, as Jabari quizzed him.

"Does it hurt? The bullet still in there? Is Mr. Benson going to jail for a hundred years?"

"Yes, a little. No and No," Larry said, chuckling. "Now finish the wonderful dinner your mother made for us."

"Well, I'm glad you're home, Daddy…" Simone said.

"Now that's what I should be hearing from my children," Larry said.

"So you can read me a bedtime story," Simone finished.

"Oh, is that all I'm good for to you?" Larry leaned over to tickle Simone, wincing a little in pain.

"Larry please, take it easy," Marian said, starting to get out of her chair. "All we need is for you to fall and break your leg the day we get you back home. We missed you."

Larry looked at Marian as though deeply touched. "I missed you too, sweetheart."

Marian was glad to hear that, glad that she wasn't the only one, like she had feared. Not until her husband was taken away from her for that night did she realize what a fool she's been acting, playing games with Paul. All that would stop. She had already devoted herself to turning everything around.

This afternoon, once she had gotten her husband home, she helped him upstairs and into the bed. She took off his shoes, fluffed a pillow for behind his back and gave him the remote control.

"How's that? Need anything?" Marian asked. "I can go down and get it for you. Hungry?"

Larry reached out a hand for her. "Baby, come here."

She climbed in bed with her husband, nestled up next to him.

"What's wrong?" Larry asked.

Marian stared at her husband, wondering how he could read her so easily. She thought to withhold what she was thinking, but decided honesty was best.

"When Tatiana accused you of…you know, you told me you didn't do it. I believed you, but…there was some doubt." Marian shifted in bed, rose to her knees beside Larry. "I am so sorry for not having total faith in the fact that you were innocent. I feel terrible. Can you ever forgive me?"

Larry smiled, pressed a hand to his wife's face. "I love you. So yes, sweetheart, of course I can forgive you."

"Really?" Marian said, excited. She hugged Larry again and kissed his lips. "But I also need forgiveness for pushing a little too hard: the counselor, always taking you from your work, the awful things I said the other night after I had been drinking."

"Listen," Larry said. "The Lord says, love is patient, love is kind. It does not envy or boast. It does not delight in evil, but rejoices with the truth. It always protects always trusts, always hopes, always perseveres. Love never fails. As I know you will never fail me."

"Yes."

"You had every right to be angry. I missed our anniversary, and I missed the counseling session. So we're even."

"No we're not, and I'm going to make it up to you," Marian said, snuggling in next to Larry again. "I'm going out and getting a new bra and panty set, maybe some shower gel and a new fragrance. You know what that means, right?"

Larry smiled. "Tell me."

"That tonight, I'm going to make love to you like never before."

"Really?"

"Yes. I just want us to have dinner as a family, you and I come back up here, sex it up like we we're teenagers, and then I just want to sleep right up under you. You think you can handle that after just getting out of the hospital?"

"I think I'm healthy enough to make that happen," Larry said.

And Marian believed Larry was going to keep his promise till his cell started ringing at the dinner table. Both she and her husband looked over at the phone. She prayed that he wouldn't pick it up, but as always, he did.

"This is Bishop Lakes," he said right there at the dinner table, the kids playing in their food, not seeing how much their father taking that phone call hurt their mother.

She listened to him give short answers, nod his head, then say the words she loathed hearing.

"Okay, I'll be there shortly." He disconnected the call, looked over at Marian, and silently mouthed an apology.

Twenty minutes later, she stood with him beside the front door, begging him not to go. "What's so important that it would take you away from your family the day you get out of the hospital?"

"Church business."

"It's always church business," Marian said, feeling her temper slip away, even after she begged for forgiveness from her husband for that exact thing. "I told you what I wanted to do—to make love, to sleep next to you—and you said yes."

"Marian," Larry said, trying to touch his wife's face. She backed out of reach.

"And what about Simone? She thinks you're going to be here to read her a bedtime story."

"Who says I won't be?"

Marian stared into her husband's eyes, not liking his choice of words. He could've simply said he would be back—promised her he would, but both of them knew good and well he most likely would not be. She leaned in, kissed her husband on the cheek. "Be careful."

44

Larry let himself into Shreeva's condo, angry that she had phoned him and taken him away from dinner with his family.

"Shreeva," he called, walking slowly into the living room. The place was quiet. There were three empty bottles of liquor on the coffee table, two glasses and an ashtray full of cigar ashes. "Shreeva, you here?" Larry called again, stepping over a nightgown on the carpet. Thinking he heard movement in the bedroom, he started in that direction, but was startled when Shreeva appeared in the bedroom doorway, stark naked.

"Baby," she said, out of breath. Her eyelids hanging low, she held on to both sides of the doorframe, as though without its support, she would fall. "Baby," she said again, stumbling toward Larry.

Larry hurried to her, caught her in his arms before she fell, held her bare body close to him. "You alone?" he said, trying to look over her shoulder into the bedroom.

"You lied to me," Shreeva said, her words slurred.

"Are you alone?"

"He's gone. They mayor is gone."

Larry dragged Shreeva back into the bedroom, sat her on the edge of the bed and grabbed a robe out of the closet to cover her.

He went to the kitchen, made her coffee and forced her to drink it black.

Her hair mussed all over her head, she held the cup with both hands, taking tiny sips. After a moment, she lowered the cup from her mouth and looked up at Larry with bloodshot eyes. "You lied to me."

"What are you talking about?"

"You said he was gonna let you build that church, and that we'd—"

"He is. We had a deal."

"We were smoking and drinking," Shreeva said. "He was loaded. He started talking about you, what a clown you were, he said. He said that all the bishops and pastors in Union City hated you, and it didn't matter what he told you, there was no way he was going to allow you to finish your church."

Larry stood from the bed, infuriated. "You sure he said those things about me?"

"How am I going to be the first lady of your new church if there ain't no new church?"

"No," Larry said, pulling the cup of coffee from Shreeva. He set it on the floor then grabbed her by the shoulders. "Are you sure he said that? That there was no way he was letting me finish my church?"

"Yes, Larry! Yes! He said there was already some guy named Ridgeway hoping to takeover what you did and make that his new place."

Larry angrily paced across Shreeva's bedroom floor. "Fine. Fine! If that's the way he wants to do this." He stopped in front of Shreeva. She was bent over, her face in her hands, long strands of her hair falling over her arms.

"Tell me you had the video recorder going," Larry said.

Shreeva looked up. "Huh?"

"I said, please tell me you had the video recorder going."

Shreeva looked in the direction of a corner of the room. She appeared exhausted, on the verge of passing out. "I turned it on when he got here. I think I got him."

Larry walked over to the bookcase, removed several of the books from the third shelf, and retrieved the recorder. Shreeva had tiny video cameras installed in her condo—two in the bedroom, two in the living room and one in the bathroom. She made it a point to record many of her sessions with some of the more powerful men she gave herself to, just in case. This was one of those times Larry knew those cameras would come in handy.

Larry stopped the recorder then rewound the video, watching the tiny screen till he saw the blurred, fast moving images of the huge Mayor's naked body. He pressed pause, and yes, it was Mayor Bonner, bent over, sweating like a pig on top of Shreeva.

Larry pulled the SD card from the device, telling himself, they would see who the clown was now.

45

Lying in bed next to his sleeping wife, Van stared up at the ceiling, feeling more calm and relaxed than he had in a long time. In another five hours, Sierra would go in to work her last night shift. After that they'd be on the same schedule for the first time since they've been married. Van checked their bank account today; for the first time in so long, there was actually more than a dollar and some change in it. And most important, since he had spoken to Bishop, he hadn't been having the awful thoughts and dreams that tormented him in the past. Nor had he committed any of the gruesome acts, like in the bar with Cashmere.

Van rolled over, kissed his wife softly on the cheek, careful not to wake her. He knew that bar fiasco with Cashmere was a cry for help, a cry for attention from the man who hurt him, the man who made him feel worthless and unloved after promising Van he would never leave him. But now that he's accepted Van back, things were much better for him.

There was movement in Virgil's crib, and Van sat up to see his son standing and smiling over the railing.

"Hey little guy," Van said, climbing out of bed. "Look who's awake? Look who's up?" Van grabbed the boy up and bounced him in his arms on the way back to the bed. "Let's lay down with Mommy. Whatcha say about that?"

Van lay on his back, sitting Virgil on his chest, the infant smiling, pawing at his father's face, squeezing Van's cheeks with his little fingers.

Van thought about the night he held a gun to the boy's head. He shut his eyes tight, admonished himself for the thought, then forever put it out of his head. He was not that person anymore. He opened his eyes and smiled at his child and reminded himself that things were different now—much better. He could almost say things were great. But if that was the case, why would he tell Robby and Urail he would go along with their little plan to find dirt on Bishop?

Earlier at the bar when Robby was talking nonsense about making their gripes against Bishop official, Van said, "And exactly what do you mean by official?"

"We get a lawyer just like the girl did, and we file charges of our own," Robby said.

"Charging him with what?" Van said.

"What he did to us?" Urail said.

"That was years ago," Van said. "Would anyone believe us? And if they did, would they care? It was so long ago."

"Then we find out who he's doing it to now," Robby said.

"We do that how?" Van said, knowing Bishop had gotten help and stopped mistreating the boys who trusted and loved him. He would've told Robby and Urail that, but something told him they would believe him a trader of some kind. "How do we find out who, if anybody he's doing those things to now?" Van asked of Robby.

Robby didn't speak, seeming not to know the answer.

Van turned to Urail. "You got any ideas since Robby can't come up with nothing?"

"We follow him," Urail said, his eyes wide. "And keep following him wherever he goes till he—"

"No," Robby said. "We go where we always used to go. We go to service on Sunday, check him out. See if something—"

"No," Van said. "He told us we can't go back there."

188

"Why?" Robby said. "Because he doesn't want people to see us? Because he has something to hide?"

"Because he's hiding something," Urail said.

"Van, you're a part of this. You need to go with us. If he has nothing to hide, if he's no longer fucking over the boys he's supposed to be mentoring, then there will be no harm done."

Van stood from his bar stool, wanting to tell Robby he was wasting his time, but he wanted to be there when Robby saw that for himself—and Van did miss the church. "Fine, I'll go with you all on Sunday."

Sierra stirred beside Van, opening her eyes a little, smiling when she saw Virgil sitting on Van's chest. She grabbed the baby's foot, brought it to her face and kissed his toes. "I gotta get up for work yet?" she asked Van, trying to locate the bedside clock.

"Naw, baby," Van said. "You got lots of time before you go."

She closed her eyes, smiling wider, and asked, "You good, baby?"

Van thought for a moment, smiled himself and said, "Yeah, baby. I'm good."

46

Mayor Bonner had a big, beautiful home almost as large as the mansion Larry lived in, and almost as nicely decorated.

When Larry called Mayor Bonner and told him it was imperative they meet, Bonner said he was in for the night and had no plans of coming back out.

"I'll come to you," Larry said.

"Weren't you just shot? Shouldn't you be in bed or something?"

"This matter warrants me being out of bed," Larry said. "I promise it'll only take a minute."

Larry sat in Bonner's darkly paneled den. It was a beautiful room: an office space on one side, a rec room, complete with pool table, leather chairs, full bar and a mounted big screen TV on the other.

On the TV was a re-broadcast of the evening news. Larry sat back, out of the corner of his eyes, watching Mayor Bonner's expression go from intrigue to disappointment.

Video played of Larry alongside Attorney Michaels, Tatiana Benson and her mother outside of the Atlanta police station.

"…and I can fully understand how a man can be driven to do such a thing," Larry said during the short interview, earlier that evening. "If my daughter told me that some man put his hands on her, I would want to go after him, too. I wouldn't actually do it, because I know that all things are in the Lord's hands and He would take care of them as He sees fit. But for that reason I refuse to press charges against Mr. Benson. I want him to be able to return to his family and for them to work through this situation as best they can."

Larry turned to Bonner. "You're just seeing that?"

"I am," Bonner said, taking a gulp of the drink he had made himself before sitting down. Larry declined the drink Bonner offered to make him. "Guess you're off the hook then. And you're looking like a hero to boot. Something tells me the only reason you didn't press charges is for the good PR you'd get."

"I was never on the hook. I told you I didn't do it. And you're absolutely right. That man deserves to rot in prison for shooting me, but letting him go back to his life of poverty makes me look like a saint," Larry smiled. "The people of Union City should have no problem welcoming me into the fair town now, don't you think?"

"About that," Bonner said, setting down his glass. "I'm starting to reconsider what I told you the other day."

"You can't reconsider. The deal's made. I agreed to pay you once the church is up and running. You've already benefited from the services of my girl, so there's no reconsidering," Larry said, fighting the urge to close in on Bonner, grab him by the throat and strangle the man till his fat cheeks turned purple and he could barely breath. Bonner was trying to block the build of his church, which would take money from Larry, possibly send him back to poverty, and he would let no man force him to do the things he once had to do just to make enough to live.

Larry was fifteen years old. One night, he stood on a corner two doors down from the open door of a bar. Raunchy music and laughter spilled out of the building. Two men stood in front of that door. Larry felt uncomfortable as he watched his father talk to those men.

An hour before, Lincoln stood over Larry, looking painfully thin and exhausted. They had slept the last three nights in doorways of abandoned buildings. They had panhandled during that time, but only made enough money for food.

"You're going to be able to do this for us, right?" Lincoln said, holding Larry by the shoulders.

"I think so," Larry said, trembling, so scared he could barely speak.

The grip on his shoulders tightened, and Lincoln shook his son. "You can't think, Larry! You have to know! I can't sleep on the street another night. We need a bed, some hot water to wash our asses. This is not just for me—this is for us. Can you do it?"

Larry nodded. "I can do it for us."

On the dark street, Larry watched as his father continued to speak to the two men then pointed at Larry. Both men looked up and across the street; sick smiles slowly spread across their faces as they nodded their approval.

Lincoln hurried back across the street to his son, looking uncertain now—looking as frightened as Larry felt. Lincoln pointed toward the two men. He bent over, kissed his son on the cheek, then said, "I need for you to go with them."

Now Mayor Bonner smiled and chuckled. "No reconsidering, huh," he said, standing from his chair and rubbing a plump hand over his round belly. "I think you might have forgotten where you are, Bishop. This is not Atlanta, but Union City. And this is not your church but my house, and no one tells me what the fuck I can't do in my house. So I said I rethought what I told you and decided you are unable to build your church here. That's it. End of story. Now I'm glad to see you survived the attempt on your life, but seeing as though we have nothing more to talk about, you need to be getting the fuck out of my house, Bishop!"

"And what a nice house it is, Mayor Bonner," Larry said, slowly rising from his chair. "And what a nice family you have. The twin boys about to attend Georgetown University, and your beautiful, devoted wife of twenty-five years. You are a lucky, lucky man."

"Like I said, we're done talking, so if you'd—"

"And I assume with the election coming up in less than six months, you'll have no problem winning another term."

"Bishop, I'm not going to ask you again," Bonner said, stepping toward Larry as though he was going to grab him by the scruff of his shirt and toss him out.

"That is, if no one see this," Larry said, pulling out the portable recorder from his suit jacket pocket. He had the video cued up to the precise spot he wanted Bonner to view. Larry pushed the play button and held it up so Bonner could see the small screen. Bonner's large office filled with the sound of Shreeva screaming and Bonner grunting and moaning in the fit of passion.

"Turn that down!" Bonner said, grabbing for the recorder.

Larry pulled it from his reach, letting the video continue to play, but turning the volume down to a whisper.

"I'm building my church in Union City or this goes to the press, every news channel, and oh yeah, I'll personally hand deliver a copy to your wife, Eva. Do we understand each other, Mayor?"

Bonner clenched his teeth and sighed loudly. "Yes."

"And I've been doing some reconsidering of my own. That extra money we agreed I was to pay you. You'll be getting half of it."

"What? You can't do—"

"I just did," Larry said. "But that's not all. I need an interest-free government loan to complete the build of the church."

"Lakes, you're going too far!"

"Maybe, but would you rather the world see your sagging fat ass on TV?" Larry said. "Or do we have a deal?"

47

Marian lay in bed holding her cell phone. She thought only twice of calling her husband, asking when he would return home, but she knew that would only make him angry. She could not be scolded, made to feel like a child by him again without snapping back and saying something she would probably regret.

She had promised to be better, but that was with the belief that Larry would make the same effort. Earlier, he jumped after the first phone call that asked him to. He must've thought to hell with her, with the children, and with the fact that he was neglecting his family. None of that seemed to matter when someone from the church called saying they needed him.

She stared at her cell phone and thought about logging on to her email, see if there was any activity on her husband's cell phone. Estelle told Marian she would be able to see all his activity: phone calls, emails, text messages. She would even be able to track his location.

Marian imagined herself bent over her cell phone in her dark bedroom, the glow of the screen on her face as she sifted through all his business, then hurt and horrified by what she found, she'd run to her car in her robe and track him to wherever he was at that moment.

Marian wasn't that woman. Had never been that woman, and other than him running out on church business all the time, Marian had no real reason to think monitoring his every move was necessary.

Honestly, she was more pissed about the lack of sex than about Larry taking off every now and again.

She set her phone on the nightstand and clicked off the bedside lamp, trying to push all of it out of her head.

This was not the time to be doing arithmetic, but she quickly counted the days and determined it was going on four months since she had sex.

She pressed a pillow between her knees and started to grind against it.

"Stop it!" she demanded, but found herself pulling down one of the straps of her nightgown. She rubbed her breast, knowing that it was foolish to tease herself, especially sine her husband was no longer giving her sex. She needed to just go to sleep.

Marian lowered her hand, despite how good her self-massage felt, and yanked the pillow free from between her thighs. She turned, looked at the bedroom clock. It was almost 11 o'clock at night.

She grabbed her phone, deciding she would call her husband. Yes, he had an obligation to the members of his church, but his obligation to her should've been stronger.

She was about to tap the screen to ring Larry's number when her phone vibrated with an incoming text. Marian sat up, opened the tiny envelope, hoping it was from Larry, telling her he was on his way home.

SORRY ABOUT YESTERDAY. I DIDN'T MEAN TO DO ANYTHING WRONG.

The text wasn't from Larry, but Paul. He must've still been hung up about the incident in the dressing room, even after she went off on his ass yesterday.

Marian stared at the text, unable to stop herself from being transported back to that moment at Neiman's, standing in the mirror, her

196

breasts exposed, seeing Paul behind her, his dick hard, pushing into his pants. If he was lying in bed with her tonight she was sure he would've rolled her over, spread her thighs, hoisted her ass just a little in the air and—

"Stop!" She scolded herself, still staring at the message, wondering how to respond, or if she should respond at all. It was late. Answering would give Paul the wrong impression. But she was alone in bed, her thighs bared, her nipples hard and her husband who knew where.

TOLD YOU NOT TO WORRY. IT'S OK.

Marian wrote. She thought to press the send button, then decided to add…

WHAT ARE YOU DOING?

She waited for a response. Paul didn't answer. Marian glanced again at the phone wondering if *she* had done something wrong. She decided to put down the cell when it vibrated in her hand with an incoming message.

I'M IN BED. THINKING ABOUT U.

Marian felt a chill shiver through her thighs. That was a bad thing. She could imagine where this would lead if she let it. End this now, Marian told herself. She wanted to put the phone down, but found herself foolishly tapping the screen of her phone.

WHAT R U THINKING ABOUT ME?

The response said—

THINKING ABOUT HOW GOOD YOU LOOKED THE OTHER DAY AT NIEMAN'S. IT HAS ME EXCITED.

"Fuck!" Marian whispered. The image of him popped into her head again. She was still able to feel the thickness of Paul's manhood in

197

her hand. This was all wrong, but Marian couldn't keep herself from being turned on. What the hell, she thought. She was alone in her home and he was all the way at his place. Nothing could really happen.

REALLY? ARE YOU PLEASURING YOURSELF?

Marian stared at that message a long time, trying to decide if she should send it. Her mind told her no, but her dripping pussy demanded that she play this out. She pressed SEND then waited impatiently for the reply.

The response came quickly—

YES.

Paul's answer had Marian gasping for air. She was doing this, had gone this far and couldn't turn back. She thought to call him—hear his voice on the phone as he stroked his long, brown shaft. She would pleasure herself, explode, relieve her tension, allowing her to go to sleep, and she would never mention this to him again. Instead, Marian wrote…

I WANT TO SEE IT. SEND ME A…

She was going to write PIC, but at the last moment wrote…

…VIDEO. I WANT TO SEE YOU CUM.

A moment after the text was sent Marian wished she could draw it back in. She felt so humiliated at the thought of him reading what she had written, especially after how she had scolded him so many times for making advances toward her. She had gone too far. He would be appalled, save the text, show it to her husband, and then Lord only knew her terrible fate.

Marian tried to think of something to write him to explain the explicit text, but nothing came to mind. It could not be undone. Feeling as though she had made a grave mistake, Marian set the phone on her nightstand, turned off her lamp, pulled the comforter over her shoulder, rolled on her side and tried to fall off to sleep.

Not two minutes later, her phone vibrated again.

Marian peeked out over the comforter to see the little red light blinking in the dark, urging her to read the text. She didn't move. She knew Paul had written something scathing back to her, something about how her husband was going to hear about this.

She had to face it sometime. She grabbed the phone, checked the message and saw that it was not a text, but a video clip. She quickly clicked on it, and what filled the entire screen of her phone was a blurred still image of a huge penis, a fist wrapped around it, the PLAY icon waiting to be pushed.

Marian glanced at the bedroom door then thumbed the arrow. The screen came to life, Paul's hand gliding up and down the shaft of a very shiny, thick and long dick. In the background she heard him moaning, calling what she thought was her name.

No, this couldn't be happening, Marian thought, as she found herself thoughtlessly lying back, spreading her thighs, massaging her clit with her fingers. She held the phone over her, marveling at the size and beauty of the man's dick. As he stroked harder and faster, she heard his breaths quicken and she knew he was nearing the point of release. She too rubbed herself with more purpose. And then, seconds later, she felt her entire body tingle, her toes go numb as her body started to give. Finally she exploded feeling an orgasm so long suppressed and so supremely powerful and satisfying that she almost blacked out. She cried out as did he on the video, the two of them groaning, moaning and gasping in unison. And as she came, she kept her eyes glued to the phone's screen, watching the thick, white fluid spill out and ooze down alongside his throbbing dick.

The video stopped a second later. "Thank you," Marian whispered, breathing heavily. She dropped the phone onto the sheets somewhere beside her, closed her eyes and went to sleep.

48

Inside the W hotel room, Larry sat on the floor with Omar. A serving tray with a bottle of wine and some half-eaten room service sat between them.

Larry poured their glasses full of wine once again and passed one to the boy. Larry smiled as he raised his glass for a toast. "To…good company." But what Larry was actually toasting was his victory over that fat slob of a mayor, Bonner. He loved so much the look of both shock and defeat on the man's face after seeing that video and knowing he could do nothing but what the fuck Larry told him to do.

In the back seat of the Bentley, Larry texted Omar, asked him if he wanted to get together. It was after 11 p.m., but he figured the boy was still up and alone in the house. Larry was right.

Omar raised his glass, touched the rim to Larry's, drank two huge gulps and smiled drunkenly.

The only light in the room came from out the bathroom door, opened just a bit. To Larry, the boy looked so innocent with his big brown eyes, smooth skin, and pink lips.

"I watched the news, and I know Tatiana said she did it because she was having hard times, but there are a lot of people having a hard time. They don't go and accuse folks of molesting them. Things are tough for me and my mother, but I wouldn't do what Tatiana did to you."

Larry drank from his glass again, set it down. "You never told me about what you and your mother are going through. Is it money?"

"I'm kinda embarrassed to say, but yeah."

Larry scooted over closer to Omar. "Things were difficult for me and my father when I was growing up. We were very, very poor. I can't stand the thought of you going through what I did." Larry reached over, lay a hand on Omar's. "Does your mother need money?"

Omar sighed, threw his head back and covered his face in shame.

"It's okay," Larry said, squeezing Omar's hand. "It's nothing to feel bad about."

"I don't like to say, but yeah, we really need it," Omar said, unable to look Larry in the eyes.

"Don't be ashamed. I understand. I can help you."

Omar wiped at his eyes and smiled. "You're so nice to me."

"It's easy being nice to nice people." Larry grabbed the bottle of wine. "More?"

"Yeah, sure," Omar said, his eyelids heavy over his eyes. He held out his glass.

Larry filled them both. He drank, watching the boy over the rim of his glass, gulp the wine as though it was water.

"Do you work out?" Larry said, feeling lightheaded.

"Yeah, a little, I guess," Omar blushed

"Do you mind me saying that you have a beautiful body?"

"No, I guess it's cool," Omar smiled, but uncomfortably.

"You mind me saying that I want to see it?"

"What do you mean, see it?"

"Can you take off your clothes so I can see your body?"

Omar seemed all of sudden to sober up. He appeared confused. He set his glass down and stood up from the floor. "Bishop, I think maybe we should—"

"I'm not asking you for anything more than just for you to take off your clothes, let me see your body. You don't think it's worth it?"

"Worth what?"

Children today, Larry thought. He considered telling Omar that there should be nothing he shouldn't consider doing for his mother, which made Larry think about the acts he performed to help his father.

The two men Lincoln arranged for Larry to go with had taken him to a car parked behind the bar—a station wagon—where they all crowded into the backseat. Larry sat between the two of them; they reeked of alcohol and cigarettes. He watched as one of them, the thinner man with a spotty beard and bad teeth, unbuckled his pants and pulled them down to just below his waist. He grabbed his flaccid penis and began stroking it into an erection.

Disgusted, Larry turned his eyes away, looked out the window, wondering where his father was, wishing he could be with him.

"Hey!" the man on the other side of Larry said. "Get to it."

There was no sign of Lincoln. Larry knew he was alone, that his father would not save him from this, because his father put him there. They needed the money, Lincoln kept telling him. Larry needed to do this for them. "Where's the money?" Larry said, doing his best to toughen himself for what he had to do.

The man pulled three ten dollar bills from his pocket, pushed it into Larry's hand, which Larry quickly counted.

"Forty," Larry said, over the moaning of the man beside him, stroking himself.

"Your old man said thirty for both of us," the heavier man said.

"He ain't doin' it. I am. Forty."

The heavy man dug deeper into his pocket, pulled out another ten and slapped it into Larry's hand. "There! Now get to sucking, motherfucker."

Larry pushed the money into his pocket, turned to the groaning, writhing man beside him, grabbed him and started the job he was paid to do.

In the dark W hotel room, Larry refocused his attention on Omar, shutting the disturbing memory out of his mind. "Don't you think doing what I asked is worth doing if it helps your mother out? The money you say you need—I think it's worth it. I would've done anything to help my father survive."

Omar looked conflicted. He walked to the windows, glanced out the curtains, then turned back to Larry. "All you want me to do is undress, and you'll help me?"

"Yes, Omar. That's all I want you to do."

"You promise?"

"I have no reason to lie."

Omar lowered his head, unbuckled his belt, unzipped his pants, then pushed them down his legs and stepped out of them, a look on his face of fear and vulnerability.

Larry nodded, and liking what he saw, he already felt himself growing in his pants. "The underwear, too."

49

The church was crowded, thousands of people packed into the sanctuary wearing their Sunday best. They sat in awe of Bishop Lakes, entranced, hanging on his every word, standing when he told them to stand, repeating words he told them to repeat, and digging in their pockets and donating every time he had the plates passed around.

Urail, Robby and Van stood out in front of the church before service, as members chatted and moved through the front door. Robby and Urail wore jeans and t-shirts; Van was the only one who wore a shirt, tie and dress pants.

For Van, the moment was surreal. His palms sweated and his knees felt weak. He knew he shouldn't have agreed to come despite how hard Robby pressed him.

"You okay?" Robby asked.

Van didn't answer the question. "This is wrong."

"We're not doing nothing but going to church like we always used to. C'mon," Robby said, shoving Van forward. "Just don't think about it."

"Just don't think about it," Urail repeated.

The three young men sat through the entire service without incident.

Bishop Lakes led the church in a final prayer, and afterward members started to rise from the pews and slowly gravitate toward the exits.

Van, Robby and Urail remained seated, waiting for the people on the end of their row to get up and file out.

"Did you see him?" Urail whispered to Van, elbowing him. "He kept looking at that boy."

Van could've easily pretended he hadn't seen what Urail was referring to and dismissed Urail's observation as just more craziness in the boy's head, but judging by the way Robby stood there, solemn faced and silent, Van knew he saw it too.

"He's messing with that boy," Urail said, excitedly, angrilly. "He's messing with him like he did us!"

"Okay, okay, Urail," Van said, grabbing one of his wrists, fearful that the boy was going to shoot up and run after Bishop to confront him.

"He's right," Robby said. "He was damn near fucking him with his eyes."

"I wouldn't say all that," Van said.

"What we gonna do now?" Urail said.

"Nothing, remember?" Van said. "We just here going to church. Not here to do anything."

The row of members were up and moving now.

"C'mon, guys," Van said. "Let's just get out of here."

Walking very close together, bumped by the herd of church members all around them, moving toward the door, Van glanced at Robby. He looked as unsettled as Van felt. As Urail continued on ahead of them, Van said softly to Robby, "I think the bishop might have seen us."

"Uh, uh. No," Robby said, continuing to march with the crowd toward the exit, not twenty feet away from them. "I don't think he saw us during service, but now he's right there at the front door, staring me in the face."

Van quickly looked in that direction, saw that what Robby said was true.

Bishop was shaking hands, smiling, patting backs, and bidding farewell to his members as they passed him, but he was eerily staring at Robby, Urail and Van as they approached.

Urail abruptly stopped when he saw Bishop's eyes on him. "What do we do?"

Robby pushed Urail in the back, forcing him to continue. "You keep on walking. We gonna walk right past him. He ain't gonna do nothing to us. He can't no more."

Van continued forward, forcing himself to believe what Robby said was true, but having a hard time doing that. Urail walked behind him, Robby right behind Urail, a hand on his shoulder, steadily pushing him forward.

Three feet from Bishop, Van saw the man look him in the face, appearing as though he was about to speak. Van quickly turned his eyes down, continued moving past him as though he had never met the man. He was just about out the front door when he heard Urail yelling behind him.

He turned to see Robby wrestling Urail, fighting to hold him back, as Urail angrily clawed and grasped at Bishop.

"You gotta tell them what you did to us!" Urail screamed, drawing members of the church around him to see what was happening. "You gotta tell them that—"

Van ran back, grabbed Urail and helped Robby drag him out of the church.

Inside Robby's Jeep, Robby yelled at Urail. "What the fuck was that?"

Van sat in the passenger seat, Urail in the back, his forehead pressed to the window.

"I said what the fuck was that?"

"He needs to tell what he did to us!" Urail said, turning to his friends. There were tears running down his face.

"Told you, we should've never come out here," Van said. "We need to just let this die. It's over."

"Really?" Robby said. "It's over. Being in that church again, seeing him again ain't remind you of all the filthy, nasty things he did to us? And you saying it's over. You see the way he was looking at that boy, all during the service, just staring at him? You know either he already got to him or he's working on it, just like he did us, and you say this is over?"

"Yeah, that's what I say," Van said.

"No!" Urail said, smearing tears from his cheeks. "It can't be over. He's gotta tell."

"How you think you ever gonna make him do that?" Van said. "Tell me!"

Everyone inside the Jeep was silent till Robby said, "If Bishop is really messing with that boy, we get him on our side. Maybe he can get us some proof or something."

"How you gonna do that? We don't even know the kid," Van said.

Again, silence.

"There he is, right there!" Urail said, reaching up over the seat, grabbing Robby by the shoulder, stabbing his finger repeatedly into the windshield.

Van was sad to see that Urail was right. The boy that Bishop had given so much attention to during his sermon was walking across the parking lot, in his slacks, shirt and tie, away from the church.

"Okay, so what?" Van said. "What do we do?"

"We get him!" Robby said, starting the Jeep and rolling off slowly in the direction of the boy.

"What the hell are you doing?" Van said.

"We need to talk to him," Robby said, slowly following behind the boy as he walked down the sidewalk. "So we're gonna grab him."

"Grab him? What? Kidnap him?" Van said.

Robby pulled the Jeep to a stop sign some fifteen feet ahead of the direction the boy was walking. He shifted the Jeep in park, and looked over at Van. "Call it whatever you want, but we need to talk to him."

"No! Un uh!" Van said. "I ain't doing it. We don't have to do it."

"We do, in order to know for sure."

"I know for sure," Van said, tired of withholding the information he knew could put to rest the foolishness they were about to engage in. "Because Bishop told me."

Robby yanked the key from the ignition and turned to Van, disbelief on his face. Van also felt the heat from Urail's stare coming from the back seat.

"What?" Robby said. "You spoke to him?"

"You talked to Bishop?" Urail said.

"When?" Robby frowned. "What did he say?"

"Couple days ago," Van said. "I needed to know if he molested that girl. He said he didn't do it, which we know is true by what was on the news. Then he told me that he knows now what he did to us was wrong, and—"

"And he's saying it now?" Robby said. "It's too fucking late now!"

"And…" Van said. "He told me he's not doing that anymore. He got help. He's not—"

"He's lying!" Urail yelled.

"He swore to God," Van said.

"Then he's lying to God. We grabbing that kid, and then we'll know for sure," Robby said, more determined than before.

"I ain't doing it," Van said.

Robby turned to Urail. "You gonna help me grab this boy, Urail?"

Urail nodded, eagerly.

"Van," Robby said, turning to him. "I'm getting that kid in this Jeep and talking to his ass. Help us and we'll probably be able to get him in without anyone really noticing what we're doing. Punk out, and we'll probably make a scene out there, somebody might call the police, and well... either way you're apart of this. So what's it gonna be?"

Van didn't have to take too much time to think about his options. "Fuck it!" Van said, knowing what Robby said was true. Even though he believed Bishop had changed, Van was part of this. He might as well get proof that what the man told him is true.

"Let's just get this over with," Van said.

50

"Jabari, take your sister in the house, and you two change out of your church clothes," Marian said. "I'll be in shortly."

Jabari climbed out of the Town Car, taking his little sister by the hand.

"Goodbye, Paul," Simone said.

"Bye Simone, see you later Jabari," Paul said, looking over the seat and waving at the kids.

Marian pulled the door closed. They were parked in the circular driveway in front of the mansion.

Marian stared at the back of Paul's head, thinking to speak, to address what had happened last night—try to explain away her reason for requesting a video of his dick, but could not find the words. She was angry for succumbing to her need for attention—her need for sex. If Larry had been there like he should've, he probably wouldn't have given her sex, but at least his presence would've stopped her from toying with the help.

Larry hadn't crept into the house until well after midnight. Of course that woke Marian up, but unlike the other times when she considered questioning him about his whereabouts, this time she realized there was no point. He obviously didn't feel their bed was where he wanted to be, and didn't care to inform her of where he'd rather spend his time.

"I'm sorry," Marian said to Paul, deciding that was a good place to start in attempt to repair the damage she had done.

Paul turned to face Marian. "About what?"

"Don't pretend. About last night. That's not who I normally am. You have to understand, and I know I shouldn't be telling you this; it's not like it's any of your business, but my husband and I haven't been together in months."

"You don't have to explain," Paul said. "And you don't have to apologize. You did nothing wrong."

"The text messages?" Marian asked, worried.

"I deleted them."

She relaxed with a sigh, lowering her eyes. When she looked up, she saw that Paul was still staring at her in the rearview. "What is it, Paul?"

"I need to ask you something. Can I come back there?"

"No, you cannot come—"

But Paul had already pushed open his door and was stepping out the car to climb into the backseat with Marian.

Marian slapped a hand over the button, locking her door. Paul simply pressed the UNLOCK button on the key fob, unlocking it again, then slid into the back seat and closed them in together.

"You shouldn't have done that," Marian said, turned on by the feeling of being imprisoned back there against her will. "We're parked in front of my house. My husband—"

"Is still at church, and will be there another couple of hours."

Marian looked out the darkly tinted windows of the big sedan at the three acres of land the mansion was built on. It wasn't like they were parked on the street and passersby would witness Paul in the back seat with her. And yes, Larry wouldn't be home for another couple of hours, if he came home that early. "Tell me what you have to say, Paul, before someone comes out here and finds us."

Paul was silent for a moment. He stared out the front windshield, then turned to Marian and said, "You told me this time and time again. We have only a professional relationship. I work for you. You tell me what to do and I'm supposed to do it. So...so tell me whatever you need from me and I'll do it."

"I don't know what you're talking about, Paul."

"In the time I've worked for you, I've gotten a crush on you, developed feelings...I don't know. But I do know nothing real will ever come of it, but I don't like to see you suffering."

"I'm not suffering," Marian said, insulted by the idea of Paul feeling pity for her.

"Fine," Paul said. "I hate to see you going without what you need, what you should be getting. So I'm telling you that if you find yourself needing an outlet, a release—use me. Tell me what you need and I'll do whatever you want."

Marian shivered against the thought, and squirmed a little on her seat, trying to stop the tingling in her panties. "I think we should stop this conversation."

"We don't have to really even do anything. We can just talk...whatever you need."

Marian stared at Paul, unable to believe what he was saying. But what was even more unbelievable was that she was actually considering his offer. He stared back at her, nothing but seriousness on his face.

"What happened last night, did that help?"

Marian blushed, turned her eyes from Paul when she said, "I guess."

"Did you like what you saw?"

Caught off guard, Marian burst with laughter. "No. I'm not answering that."

"My phone is kinda old," Paul joked. "The video on it is real grainy. Could you make it out okay?"

Still blushing, unable to beat down the stupid girly grin on her face, Marian said, "I told you, I'm not messing with that."

"That means you couldn't really see it good. But since we're here, you might as well see what it looks like in real life," Paul said, unzipping his pants.

"No!" Marian said, reaching out, trying to stop his hand. It was too late. He had already exposed his stiff penis, and she had grazed the very tip of it, trying to pull her hand back. She turned away from him and with that same hand, covered her eyes. "Paul, put that thing away!"

"Mrs. Lakes, you already saw it. You can look at it."

"Put it away. My kids could come out here."

"The doors are locked and all the windows are tinted. Look at me."

"Paul, why are you doing this?"

"We aren't doing anything. Please, can you just look at me?"

Marian took a deep breath in, exhaled then slowly turned around to face Paul. She forced herself to look directly in his eyes, and not let them stray anywhere else. "What do you want?"

"This is not about me. I'm just saying, if you ever get to that point where you need something, anything at all, you can call me. Okay."

"Okay, but I won't be calling for anything like that."

"Fine," Paul said, showing that perfect smile. "Now since I have it out, don't you wanna take a look at it?"

"No," Marian said, even though she was the slightest bit curious.

"So what are you thinking, that if you do, then you won't be able to help yourself and you might do something crazy?"

"Not at all. My resolve is rock solid."

"Then just look."

"Fine," Marian said. She let her eyes fall, and what she saw was a perfectly shaped, brownish pink penis, the length, girth and curve of an enormous banana. She gasped, but could not take her eyes away. "I need to go."

"Give me your hand first."

Marian didn't ask why. She was already in too deep. She turned her face away from him and slowly gave over her hand to him. She felt him take it, then place her palm against his incredibly warm dick, and slowly wrap her fingers around it. She let it sit there at first, as though it wasn't her hand at all. But then she felt herself squeezing him. What expanded in her hand was strong. It throbbed, beat, like there was a pulse running through it, and she could not help but wonder if it would feel as good inside her as it felt against her palm. She wanted to let him go, but found herself slowly starting stroke him as he had himself in the video he sent her last night.

She heard him release a slight groan. "Mrs. Lakes, what are you…"

"Be quiet, Paul," Marian told him, trying to concentrate on what she was doing. She continued massaging him with one hand, the other, she brought to her mouth, licked her palm, coating it with saliva, then grabbed him with both hands, gliding them up and down his dick. Paul writhed about, gripping the leather seats, moaning heavily.

"I'm gonna…I'm gonna…" he panted.

"Come!" Marian said, grabbing tightly to his balls with one hand, gliding her palm over the head of his dick with the other. She felt him ready to explode, to give in to her. "Yes, come for me! Come!"

As if obeying her command, Paul cried out and spilled his warm, thick fluid out over her hands, as she continued to pump out every drop. She watched his body convulse, his hands reach for her, then pull, as he gently bit down on his full, bottom lip. She could've imagined kissing him that moment, but that wasn't what this was.

She snatched a few sheets of Kleenex from the box sitting on the center console between the seats, and wiped her hands, then said, "I'll let you know what I decide about your offer. Till then, take the rest of the day off."

51

The restaurant where Shreeva worked as a hostess was packed for a Sunday night. Shreeva was off, so Larry treated her to dinner, along with Tyrell Suggs, and James Cunningham, a stout, red haired middle-aged white guy. He was the owner of the construction company building Larry's new church.

Their table was littered with the remnants of what they had eaten and drank: plates of half eaten entrees and appetizers, three empty bottles of wine, one still half full, and several empty shot glasses.

"A toast," Larry said, raising his wine glass.

Tyrell Suggs, Shreeva and James Cunningham, all raised their glasses, waiting to hear what they were toasting.

"The Lord is my refuge and my fortress, my God, in whom I trust. I'm so glad he delivered me from all that mess," Larry said.

"Amen!" Shreeva said.

"And to getting back to building my church. It's been on hold too, too, too long," Larry added, his speech slurring.

"Amen to that," James Cunningham said.

They all brought their glasses to their lips and drank. Larry lowered his, elated, thinking he would order another, then told himself he wouldn't. He knew he had far too much already for he believed he saw, standing before him, one of the boys that visited him at church earlier today. Larry attempted to blink the hallucination away, he rubbed his eyes a moment, but the image of the boy wearing the rain boots, and winter coat would not disappear. Only when Larry heard him speak did he realize his imagination was not playing tricks on him. Urail had somehow happened upon him, walked into the restaurant and was standing, angrily before him.

"Bishop, you have to tell what you did to us. You have to tell—"

"Larry," James Cunningham said, looking concerned. "Who is this?"

Larry laughed, quickly turned to Shreeva, and under his breath said, "Call someone over here, now!"

Shreeva stood, raising a hand, attempting to flag down a waiter.

"You lied to us!" Urail said, raising his voice. "You told us you loved us, told us you wouldn't hurt us."

"Bishop, what you want me to do?" Tyrell Suggs said, pushing back in his chair.

"Don't do anything. Everything is going to be fine," Larry said, starting to panic, but trying not to show it.

"But you hurt me. You fucked me. Always wanted to fuck me!" Urail said, drawing the attention of other diners. They were looking in Larry's direction, chattering, gawking, standing from their chairs.

"You said you loved me!" Urail said, louder.

"Tyrell!" Larry said. "Get him!"

"Made me put you in my mouth, suck you till you did it in my mouth!"

Tyrell was up out of his chair, had grabbed Urail at the same time two big waiters had reached him. Urail fought them, wrestling them, swinging, screaming, as he was dragged out. "You gotta tell how you fucked us then kicked us out. Fucked us then left us! You gotta tell, Bishop!" Urail screamed, his high-pitched cries filling the room.

After Urail was removed, the restaurant was deathly quiet. A half dozen people stood in front of their tables, staring in Larry's direction.

Larry was infuriated, but he smiled, chuckled and said, "I have no idea who that was," Larry said, speaking to everyone, and no one in particular. He stood, raised one of the glasses on his table. "I'm sorry for the disturbance. Drinks are on me!"

The diners did not applaud Larry's gratitude like in the movies. Instead, the people who were standing lowered themselves to their seats, and those gawking simply turned their attention back to their conversations.

Larry looked across the table at James Cunningham. The man's skin looked two shades whiter than it was a moment ago.

"Everything okay, Larry?" James asked, the question filled with skepticism.

Shreeva threw an arm around Larry's shoulders, smiled seductively at James, and said, "He must've been some homeless person, half out of his mind to say those things about the good Bishop. Obviously, he doesn't know what a true pussy hound Larry really is."

52

Monday evening after work, Van sat on the stair out in front of his apartment building. He waited for the call from Robby, to find out what would happen with the boy they had all but kidnapped yesterday.

Once they forced him into Robby's Jeep, Urail and Van jumped in on either side of him in the back seat. Robby started the truck and sped off.

They boy was frightened out of his mind, yelling, fighting trying to get out of one of the Jeep doors, whipping his head back and fourth, as though afraid he would be murdered.

"Shut up! Just shut up!" Robby ordered, looking up in the rearview mirror, as he took hurried turns, tossing the four of them about the speeding Jeep.

"What are you gonna do to me? Who are you? What are you doing?" The boy screamed as Van and Urail tried to hold his arms and grab him around the shoulders.

"What are y'all doing back there?" Robby yelled. "It's two of y'all and just one of him. Can't y'all control him?"

"The boy is strong," Urail said.

It took fifteen more minutes to calm the boy and convince him that he would not be hurt. Robby stopped the Jeep in a parking lot on a desolate street and the four climbed out, Van, Urail, and Robby surrounding the boy. He finally told them his name after being asked almost a dozen times.

Robby told Omar why they grabbed him, and what they wanted to know.

"Yeah, I know Bishop Lakes. He's the bishop of the church I go to. Why?" Omar said, sounding less scared and more pissed off by what he was going through.

"He done stuff to you?" Urail asked.

"Like what? What would he be doing to me?" Omar said.

Robby stepped around Urail and Van, pushed them out the way. "Y'all pussy-footing around this thing." He turned to Omar. "Has Lakes tried to get with you?"

"What? What are you talking—"

"Nigga, don't act like you don't know. We saw the way he kept staring at you in church. Has he tried to fuck you?" Robby said.

"Oh, here we go," Van said, slapping a hand to his forehead.

Omar was silent, guilt written on his face.

"See!" Robby said, turning to Van, pointing a finger at Omar. "He has, hasn't he?"

"I don't know what you're talking about."

"You a damn lie!" Robby said, walking up on the boy, snatching him by the shirt.

Van grabbed Robby, pulled him away from Omar. "Omar," Van said, his voice calm. "We're sorry for all of this."

"Then let me go."

"We can't just yet," Van said.

"You can't or you won't?" Omar said.

"Just shut up and listen," Robby said, from behind Van.

"Omar," Van said. "This is very important. Just talk to us, and we'll drive you back to wherever you want to go. We obviously ain't trying to hurt you or we would've done that by now. Can you talk to me?"

Omar glared at the boys through uncertain and suspicious eyes. "I guess. For a minute, but I need to be going."

"Fine. Okay," Van said, seeming nervous all of a sudden. "Has Bishop Lakes ever tried to…I don't know…touch you?"

"Why are you asking—"

"You said you would talk. Talk!" Robby said.

Omar swallowed hard and lowered his head. "He's come by my house a few times. Picked me up from school. Stuff like that."

The boys drew in closer. Fearful expressions covered their faces.

"Was there anything else?" Robby asked.

"He bought me this watch," Omar said, holding it up so the boys could see.

Van knew the brand, saw the commercials. He knew they were pricey and wondered why Bishop would spend that kind of money on a boy if he no longer did what he had done to Van, Urail and Robby. His fear grew when he asked, "Other than getting you the watch, has he tried to do anything to you?"

"Why?" Omar asked.

"Because he's done some things to some boys before," Robby said. Van looked away. "Bad things, sexual things. It ruined their lives, and we don't want that to happen to anyone else."

"To what boys?" Omar said, shocked. "You all?"

"Yeah," Urail said. "He did bad things to us. He fucked us and—

"

"Shut up, Urail!" Van said.

"But he did," Urail said, stepping forward.

"Motherfucker got me, too," Robby said. "This ain't no joke, Omar. What he did to us messed us up pretty bad, and he'll do the same to you if you let him. So you need to tell us, did he do anything more than just pick you up from school, come to your house, and buy you a fucking watch?"

"How about you?" Omar said to Van. "He get you, too?"

Van had never admitted what Bishop did to him. It was a secret he promised himself he would carry to his grave. But things have changed. Van lowered his eyes and nodded his head.

Omar sighed, kicked at the ground and shook his head. "The other night he took me to some hotel in Dunwoody. He got me drunk, told me he liked my body and said he would give me some money to help my moms if I stripped down."

There it was, Van thought. After all the harm Bishop did to them, the promises he made, the love he stole, the horrific sexual acts he committed against them and made them commit, only to lie to Van, tell him that he had stopped all of that, was cured, when he knew he wasn't. Van trusted him yet again, welcomed him back into his life, was looking forward to loving the man as a father once again…but now…

"And you stripped for him? You did it?" Van asked, sadly.

"My moms, she's needing the money, and—"

"No need to explain, man," Robby said. "We all get it. Anything else happen?"

"No!" Omar said, offended.

"Not yet," Urail said.

"We trying to get him for what he's done to us, but we're gonna need some proof that he's still doing it. We gonna need you to get his voice on tape, record him asking you something, video, pictures or something," Robby said.

"What? No!" Omar said.

223

"Calm down," Van said. "You don't have to do it if you don't want to, but we haven't told you everything we have for nothing. We've been where you're heading. And you might think he's this great man, think he cares for you, loves you, and you might love him, but—"

"Love him?" Omar said, like the thought never entered his mind.

"You say it like that now," Van said. "But if you don't do what we ask you, and you keep on with him, it will happen."

"Yeah," Robby said. "He will use you in ways you'll never be able to forgive yourself for, and then he'll leave you. We don't want that to happen to you, so will you help us?"

Omar appeared scared. It was the right reaction, Van thought. It meant the boy was starting to believe them.

"I...I don't know," Omar said.

Van glanced down at his watch, wondering what was keeping Robby and Urail, when the Jeep finally pulled to the curb in front of him.

"Yo," Van said, standing. "I was just about to call you."

"Get in the truck," Robby said.

"Did you hear from Omar?"

"Van, did you hear me? Get in the fucking truck!"

Van climbed in. Robby raced off.

"What the hell is wrong with you?" Van said.

"The hospital called. Urail's in ICU. Someone damn near beat his ass to death.

"What? Who?" Van said, stunned.

Robby turned to Van. "Bishop, who else?"

224

53

It was a little after 11:30 at night and it all seemed too much for Van to bear as he tried to push the key into the lock of his apartment door. He had drunk far too much, trying to cope with the near death of his friend.

Robby and Van ended up at Grady Hospital, where they stood on opposite sides of Urail's bed. His head was bandaged up with thick white gauze. A tube snaked down his nose, another went into his vein and another was connected to a bag of piss that hung from a rail by his side. His face was discolored with bruises and inflated by swelling, making him almost unrecognizable as the somewhat handsome young man he was the day before.

"Goddammit!" Robby said, turning away from the awful sight of Urail. "He's gone too far this time. I swear we ain't gonna stop going after Bishop till we get him for this. Do you hear me, Van?"

Van stood, gently holding one of Urail's hands in his, trying not to shed a tear for his friend.

"I said do you hear me?" Robby said, angrily pacing around the room. "We don't stop till we get him!"

Afterward Robby and Van drove to the nearest hole-in-the-wall bar. They stared dumbstruck at each other, drinks in front of them, unable to believe what happened.

Van stood and stared silently at Robby.

"What?" Robby said.

"How did you find out this happened to Urail?" Van asked.

"A nurse called me. She said Urail told her my cell number." Robby shook his head. "Boy crazy as hell, ain't got a phone, but can remember my number after not talking to me for years. Who the hell does that?"

"Urail does," Van said.

"We gonna drink, or just sit here wondering why Bishop did this to our boy?"

"We need to drink," Van said, grabbing his glass. "To Urail."

The two boys drained their glasses in the small, dark bar then slammed them down, wincing against the stiffness of the alcohol.

"Why you think Bishop did this?" Van asked.

"Urail was always messing with him. He told me he went to the church to steal stuff. Security pulled him in, threatened him. He even went to Bishop's house, and that ugly motherfucker in the suits that always hangs with Bishop, told Urail he would get beat down if he is ever seen running up on Bishop again."

"Hold it," Van said. "What did you say?"

"Urail said Bishop's man threatened him. Told him that if he came to his house one more time, that if he—"

"Did Urail tell you tonight that it was Bishop or Bishop's man that did this to him?"

Robby shook his head. "He couldn't. By the time I got here, he was all drugged up and knocked out."

"Then you can't say for sure it was Bishop. We won't know that till we talk to Urail," Van said.

Robby turned to Van looking as though he wanted to fight him. "What is it always with you, always trying to defend him? Did he bend your ass over and fuck you a special way that makes you not wanna see him pay for what he did to us?"

"Fuck you, Robby," Van said, raising a hand to order another drink.

"Who else would've done it? Anyone could see plain as day Urail wasn't all there. His clothes were filthy. He ain't have no money. He never fucked with no one. Why would someone, anyone, waste the time to talk to him, let alone beat the shit out of him?"

Van slid the key into the lock then pushed open his apartment door.

He staggered in, closed the door quietly behind him and found his wife sitting on a chair in the corner of the room. She wore her security guard uniform. Van looked to his right, and Virgil was sleeping peacefully in his crib.

"I...I...can explain," Van said, holding up both hands.

Sierra stood, walked over to him, and embraced him, kissing him on the side of his face. "I'm so sorry," she said. "Robby told me what happened to Urail when he called looking for you earlier."

Van wrapped his arms around Sierra, squeezed her as tight as he could.

After their three or four drinks, Robby drove Van back to his car. They were both drunk. Staring at Van standing outside the open door of Robby's Jeep, Robby said, "We gonna get Bishop's ass for this. You hear me? I'm gonna get a lawyer, and we're gonna get his ass. But I need you to be with me. You with me, Van?"

Van stumbled a bit, straightened himself up and sadly said, "Yeah, Robby. I'm with you, and we gonna get him."

227

Van climbed into his Honda, knowing he should've been headed home, but didn't. He returned to the crowded Piedmont Park bar he was in some nights ago, where he met Cashmere. Boys sat elbow to elbow at the bar, while near deafening music played.

Van had only just finished his first drink when someone asked: "You want another?" The question came from a blonde, spike-haired man. He had to yell over the loud music playing. His name was Jacob. He was thin, and clean-shaven.

Van turned toward the fuzzy vision of the man, and smiled, even though he felt like crying, the image of Urail beaten and drugged up in that hospital, still in his head. "Okay," Van said, cupping his hands to his mouth and pressing them to the man's ear so that he could hear him. "But I have to go home after this."

"All right," Jacob said. "But you don't have to go alone if you don't want."

Sierra released Van, took a step back so she could look in his face. She saw that he was crying. "Baby," she said, hugging him again. "I'm gonna call in, tell them I can't come to work tonight."

"No," Van said. "I'll be all right. Just go."

"Your friend is in the hospital. You shouldn't be alone. I think I should just—"

Van took his wife by the shoulders, held her tight. "I'm gonna be fine. You got this one more night to work, and I don't want you messing up any chance of you getting days. Just go."

"You'll talk to me about all this tomorrow?"

"You know I will."

"And if you need anything tonight—"

"You know I'll call you," Van said.

Sierra smiled, took Van's face in her palms and kissed his lips. "Get some rest, baby. Everything is gonna work out fine, and Urail will be better soon."

Five minutes after Sierra stepped out the door, the apartment intercom buzzer rang. His head still fuzzy from the alcohol, Van staggered to the call box and pressed a button. "Yeah?"

"It's Jacob. Can I come up now?"

A minute later, Van pulled the door open to see Jacob standing there, a drunken smile on his face. "Your wife gone?"

"Yeah," Van said, feeling horrible about what he was doing, but told himself not to think about it. His best friend was in horrible condition, laid up in the hospital. The man Van thought he could trust again was nothing more than the man that had lied to him, abused and mistreated him for years. It was all too much for Van, and he just needed to kill all the guilt, remorse and anger in his head. This was the only way he knew to do that.

Jacob grabbed Van, pulled him close and tried to kiss his lips. Van turned his face away. Jacob fumbled with the button on Van's jeans, then dropped to his knees. Van pulled him back up off the floor.

"What do you want?" Jacob gasped. "You want me?"

Van's mind screamed no, but he nodded his head.

Jacob turned his back to Van, dropped his jeans and boxer shorts to his knees, then finding nowhere else, bent over, leaning his forearms against Virgil's crib. Looking over his shoulder, Jacob smiled, "C'mon. I promise I won't wake the baby."

Feeling outside himself, Van walked over, unfastening his pants. He was ready, and he hated himself for that. He grabbed Jacob roughly

229

by the hip with one hand, and with the other, unzipped his fly when he heard the apartment doorknob turning.

A second later the door opened. "Sorry, I forgot—" Sierra said, then she went mute, her eyes ballooning, the keys falling to the floor, as she stared at the two men bent over her sleeping baby's crib.

"What are you doing to my baby?" Sierra screamed, lunging at Jacob, trying to gouge out his eyes with her fingernails.

His pants still around his ankles, Jacob dodged Sierra, but managed to get scratched across his face. Two bloody lines opened up on his cheek.

"Sierra, please!" Van said, attempting to grab his wife.

Jacob, touched his face, and saw blood on his fingertips as Sierra continued to charge him. Again Jacob stepped aside, this time rearing back, throwing a punch that struck Sierra across the jaw. She stumbled backward, tripped over her feet and spiraled to the floor.

Van turned to Jacob, enraged.

"I...I didn't mean it. She was—" Jacob tried to explain.

Before he could utter another word, Van was on top of him, had thrown him to the floor, striking him over and over again with his fists. Somewhere behind him, he heard his wife screaming, but he continued punching, trying to destroy everything Jacob represented, destroy the reality of Urail being beaten, the things Bishop had done to him, the freak he had made Van into.

"Van, you're going to kill him!" Sierra screamed.

Her cry was bloodcurdling. He stopped beating Jacob, turned to see his wife kneeling on the floor behind him, terrified, her face wet with tears.

When Van turned back to Jacob, he was up, his face covered with his blood. He staggered, fell back to the floor, gathered himself, rose to his feet again, threw open the front door, and stumbled out of the apartment, noisily bumping into walls as he ran down the hallway.

Van stood staring at his wife, breathing heavily, his right fist throbbing, his knuckles smeared with blood. He just noticed that his son was screaming.

Sierra stared back at him, sobbing. She did not look disgusted by him, or by what she had just witnessed, but more disappointed, which hurt Van more for some reason.

"We were doing so good. Just please—" Van started.

Sierra quickly moved to scoop their crying child out of the crib and hurried toward the door. Their son pressed close to her breast, she stopped before opening the door and said, "I never want to see you again."

54

The next day, Robby pulled the Jeep into the parking lot of a Starbucks Coffee.

"Why you stopping for coffee?" Van said. "I thought we were supposed to be meeting some attorney."

"We are," Robby said, shutting the Jeep off and climbing out of the front seat. "We meeting her here."

"We're talking about some sensitive stuff," Van said, climbing out the Jeep. "Why don't we just meet at her office?"

Robby walked toward the store without answering. Van followed, concern on his face. "Robby, I said why don't we just meet at her office?"

Grabbing the door handle, Robby turned. "Because she don't have an office, all right! She works out of her apartment, and she thought meeting here would be better than in her damn one bedroom, okay."

Inside Starbucks, Van was grateful that at least the place was crowded. Only a few people worked on laptops at circular tables, wearing earphones and minding their own business.

Over to the left, a black woman stood from a table with four chairs. She wore a well-fitted business suit. To Van, she was attractive, but looked very young, as though she might have just graduated from law school. She held out a hand to Van.

"Hi, I'm Shelia Kennedy."

"Good to meet you," Van said, less than sincerely.

When Robby stepped in front of her, he opened his arms, as if for a hug.

"Sit down or get out," Robby," Shelia said.

"Hey, you can't blame a brotha for trying," Robby said.

"Please, everyone take a seat," Shelia said. "Does anyone want anything? Coffee, tea or something?"

Van shook his head.

"I think we just wanna get on with this," Robby said.

"Fine," Shelia said, sitting, picking up a tablet and pen off the table. "Robby told me a little bit about what's going on. What else can you tell me, Van?"

"Our friend Urail is in the hospital. Robby's thinking…that maybe Bishop Lakes might have something to do with it."

"Robby told me that Urail was showing up at the bishop's church, stealing, things like that, but that doesn't mean he hurt your friend," Shelia said.

"They threatened Urail before. He told me that," Robby said. "I know Bishop did it, or had someone do it."

"Can you prove it, Robby? Can you find proof that puts Urail and Bishop Lakes in the same place at the same time, and even if you could, can you prove that the man beat your friend, landing him in the hospital?"

"I told you what I know, what Urail told me. Why are you asking us all this?" Robby said.

"Maybe because she doesn't want the case. Or maybe she wants you to prove it, because she knows she can't," Van said. "Why did you even get her? She don't even have an office, don't look a day older than us, so obviously she don't know what she's talking about. I'm out of here." Van stood, ready to walk out the restaurant.

"Sir," Shelia said. "The reason why Robby "got" me is because he could "get" no one else. I don't know if he told you, but he went to more than half a dozen other attorneys, and was laughed out of their offices when he said he wanted to go after Bishop Larry Lakes for beating a homeless man who was mentally challenged. And I'm asking you all these questions because if we were to make believe and say this actually went to court, the defense attorney would want those same answers. Now Robby, will you please tell your friend to sit down?"

Robby looked up at Van, nodded at the chair he just vacated. "Sit down, Van. Let's get this shit done."

Van slowly took his seat. "So why did you even ask to talk to us if you don't believe Bishop did it?"

"Because Robby told me what he did to the three of you."

Van glanced at Robby as though his friend betrayed him. "Why did you tell—"

"Because I'm tired of hiding it, Van," Robby said. "And Shelia might as well know now, instead of after we start dating."

"In your dreams," Shelia said.

"Every night," Robby said, winking back.

"So Bishop Lakes did some things to us he shouldn't have a few years ago. That's how the public is gonna see it. So what?" Van said.

"So, I think there's enough to bring charges against him for that. I would have to get more information, though."

"But you're the one saying that we need all this proof," Van said. "Proof for this, proof for that. We ain't got no proof. We were just three kids who got taken advantage of—victims. So the fuck what?"

Shelia looked at Van as though she had reached the limit of what she would tolerate from him. "You're not just victims, you're also witnesses. You are the proof, and if you testify, I can almost guarantee you, if what you're saying is true, we'll get him for what he did to you."

55

When the Bentley pulled to the curb in front of Van's apartment building, he stepped off the curb and into the backseat.

Earlier, Van had given that young attorney Shelia Kennedy a hard time, but after she got the facts from him and Robby, she actually sounded like she knew what she was doing. She sounded as though she really cared what had happened to him, Urail and Robby, and seemed as determined as they were to get Bishop for abusing them.

Van came home after the meeting, sat in his apartment alone, hoping that Sierra would walk through the door with their son, but he knew better. Van had so much to blame Bishop for, now he had the loss of his family.

Sitting on the let-out sofa, Van dialed a number on his phone, and placed it to his ear. When the phone was picked up, Van said, "Bishop, I really need to talk. Can we meet?"

Inside the back seat of the Bentley, Van took a moment to just stare at Bishop. The man stared back at Van, smiled and said, "So you called and said you needed to meet. What's on your mind?"

"Urail's in the hospital. Somebody beat him pretty bad."

"Oh my God," Larry said. "How…how did it happen?"

"You know. You did it, or you had it done, didn't you?"

"Van, what are you talking about? Are you feeling all right?" Bishop said, scooting closer to Van. "Do you need—"

Van edged away from him. "I don't need nothing from you. You've ruined my life."

"What has gotten into you? Maybe I can help you—"

"You know my wife left me last night," Van said, ignoring Bishop. "She walked in the apartment and…and caught me about to fuck some dude. Can you help me with that?" Van asked, wiping a tear from his cheek. "What do you think, Bishop? You threw a fucking march, telling people you could help them if they were uncertain about their sexuality. Can you help me? I love my wife and child, but I was about to fuck some dude in his ass. Am I straight or a faggot, Bishop? Can you cure me of what you made me into?"

"Van, I think it's time you leave," Bishop said. "I think you have a lot on your mind and a lot to deal with, but everything is going to be fine for you."

"Oh, I know it will. Because I'm not gonna let the memory of you fuck up my life anymore. I'm gonna get my family back, and I'm gonna get past you. And like you said, everything will be all right…for me. But not for you."

"What are you talking about, son?"

"I loved you. You were the only father I knew, and I did everything to please you; every little sick, slimy sexual thing you wanted, I foolishly did, because I didn't want to disappoint my father. But I know who you are now, who you really are, and you're nothing but

237

a liar," Van said, more tears spilling from his eyes. "You haven't changed. You're still fucking boys who trust you, and you beat up my friend, Urail. And you're gonna pay for all of that."

Bishop looked threatened for the first time during the conversation. "What do you mean, pay?"

Van smeared the tears from his cheeks. "Sometimes when I think about you, I realize I still love you. Sometimes I hate you, but not enough, I guess, to stop myself from doing you a favor and warning you that me, Robby and Urail are coming for you. We got a lawyer, we gonna file suit, and unlike Tatiana, we ain't lying, and we ain't gonna lose."

"Son, you don't know what you're doing. Just calm down, and we can—"

"No," Van said, pushing the door of the Bentley open, and stepping out into the street. But before he closed the door, he said, "Seriously, Bishop, get your shit together, cause the man who's gonna get fucked this time is you."

END 4/29/31

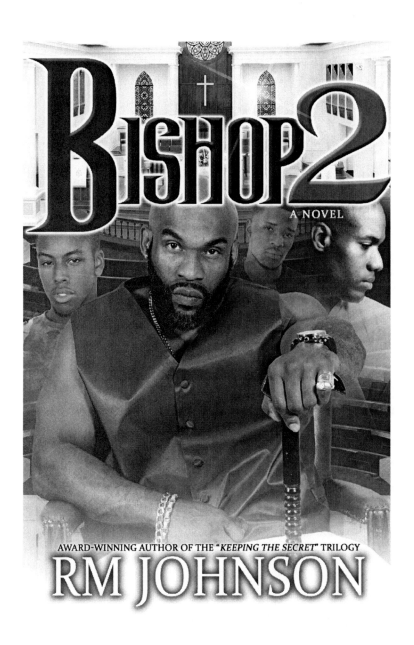

BISHOP 2

A NOVEL

AWARD-WINNING AUTHOR OF THE *"KEEPING THE SECRET"* TRILOGY

RM JOHNSON

NOW AVAILABE ON AMAZON.COM

Just enter BISHOP 2 by RM Johnson in the search box.

RM Johnson is the award-winning author of sixteen or seventeen novels. He keeps forgetting exactly how many. They include the bestselling Harris Men series, The Million Dollar and The Keeping the Secret series. He holds an MFA in Creative Writing and currently resides, happily, in Atlanta, Georgia.

RM Johnson would love to hear your comments.

Email RM at **RMnovels@yahoo.com**

Please visit him at his website: **RM-Johnson.com**

Friend him at **Facebook.com/RMnovels**

Follow him at **Twitter.com/marcusarts**

Can't get enough of RM? Why not start the wildly popular **Keeping the Secret** series for FREE!

If you leave a review of Bishop on Amazon.com, RM will send you a copy of Keeping the Secret, the first book in the series, for free!

Just email RM at rmnovels@yahoo.com, write KTS Special Offer in the subject box, and he will send you **Keeping the Secret** along with simple instructions to download it to your Kindle.

Thanks for purchasing Bishop, and thanks for your review!

CPSIA information can be o
Printed in the USA
LVOW12s2144030216

473535LV00001

9 511407